HELL HATH NO FURY

Dixie Carlton

For Nix and Alex
My best work so far...

CONTENTS

Please note – These are based on Southern Hemisphere seasons

PROLOGUE

She looked out the window at the river traffic and wondered what might be happening in a room, in a hospital nearby? Knowing all the characters in the play, she could imagine the scene unfolding and hesitated to dwell on the pictures in her mind, and yet could barely drag her imagination away from the scene.

First there would be Brett, visibly upset by the state of the woman in the bed. He had lived for nearly ten years in her home, as her friend and supporter. They had laughed, cried over movies together, battled about what he or she might be cooking for dinner, and hugged and made up many times in those years. He could barely face her frail form, knowing the end was near.

Deanna was tough, and had a hard edge to her jaw that had most likely developed as a result of all the times she stuck her chin out defiantly at her mother. Now as she neared forty, Deanna's stubborn streak was tempered a little, but she could still be a demanding and controlling woman. She would be asking the doctor about adjusting her mother's medication to make her more comfortable.

The doctor would be shaking his head and looking down at his notes, he'd make a quick remark that was neither encouraging nor supportive. Fortunately he would not see the flash in her eyes that would have made anyone else in the room step back in anticipation of an explosion. The other man in the room would grab Deanna's arm to pull her back from the flash of temper he knew was coming through years of knowing and observing her behaviour.

He would look at her, shaking his head imperceptibly to warn her to calm down, and then address the doctor. "So how long do you think this will take? Are we talking hours or days?

James was ready for whatever the answer was – he just wanted this to be over. He was willing to spend whatever it took, to ensure his wife was comfortable, and felt well-loved and nurtured to the end of her life, but he was torn between that desire, and the need to move on with his life. For three long years he had been trapped by his wife's illness, and was ready for this to be over. Finally now, they had come to this point yet again and the waiting was becoming unbearable.

The woman's eyes flicked over the river as she watched the water taxi pull up to the jetty and passengers disembark. Yes, she knew without even having to be there, exactly what would be going on in the hospital room. Having endured her own part of the drama that fortunately ended only a few days earlier, she was also impatient for this to be over. But for her, the only thing she could do was to send healing wishes to all concerned and wait for the news to come. Being there with the other main players in this drama as it ended, was not an option.

PART

ONE

The Decline

Spring, 2007

CHAPTER 1

James looked up from washing the wheels of his 1971 Mustang convertible and waved to Don next door who had just finished mowing the lawns. Don was also in his late forties, tanned and trim from running marathons, and had recently started shaving his head. In fact, as James looked at him now, he could see barely any hair on his body at all apart from his eyebrows, and who knew what might be below his waistband. He shook his head to dispel the image and instead sent his mind off in the direction of assumptions about Don and Mary's marriage.

He did that a lot lately – wondered about other couples and the state of their relationships. Well – who knew what really went on behind closed doors? he thought to himself for the thousandth time. He was a great example of that notion. Still, he thought, it's nice to contemplate happy ever afters do actually exist, and Don and Mary certainly seemed pretty happy. He'd even heard sounds of them having late night sex under the stars a few weeks earlier and it sure sounded like they were happy enough then.

Ahh – sex outdoors… what a lovely idea. He allowed himself to imagine just for a moment or two what it might be like to be plunging into the warm depths of Mary's pleasure on a warm summer's evening after skinny dipping in their pool. He was jolted out of the thought by Don calling out to him and quickly stood up, careful to take his mind off the beginnings of an unwelcome erection. Later, he mentally promised himself, and smiled at his neighbour.

"Well that's a job well done for another week or so", he said casually. "But feel free to bring your mower over and do mine if you are really keen." Don laughed and shrugged his shoulders.

"I would be happy to my friend, but you see, I think I just ran out of gas – again." laughed Don. It was a bit of an old and very rusty joke between them that still made for the start of an easy over the fence conversation that sometimes extended to sharing a few beers on the back porch of one or other of their homes.

"I think we're overdue for a cruise in that beautiful beast again, don't you?" suggested Don. They occasionally also drove James's Mustang down to the beach and had a swim after their weekend chores. Even if it was only to see if they could still get any pretty girls to look at them. Or at least they hoped that pretty girls might be attracted to the car, even if they only saw the two middle aged men in it. Not that either of them would really know what to do with such an opportunity had it ever presented itself.

The two friends had much in common – both having immigrated to Australia fifteen years earlier, and bought homes side by side when the neighbourhood was still under construction. Don having come from South Africa, and James from New Zealand. Both had been married to their respective second wives Mary and Alice for exactly twenty years, and both couples were childless, aside from

Alice's daughter Deanna, now in her mid-thirties. The two men had always got on well, whereas Mary and Alice tolerated each other out of polite consideration to their men and their close proximity to each other.

"Well that's a great idea, let's do that – say give me ten minutes to finish the tyres ok." said James.

"Righto."

James bent behind the car again and finished the task of polishing the mag wheels of his pride and joy, and was ready moments later when Don bounded over the fence and climbed into the car. The top was down, and the car turned over smoothly and purred like only a V8 could as they backed out of the driveway. Flooring the pedal as they turned the corner, of the street James felt the familiar surge of excitement the car gave him; it always got him in his balls. "Well I gotta get my thrills somewhere these days aye old girl?" he quietly thanked the car for the joy she gave him.

"What was that you say?" Don leaned closer to hear what James had said, but James just laughed and shook his head.

A little while later, as they sat on a bench seat drying off in the sun, water bottles in hand, James decided to ask his friend a question he'd been mulling over for a very long time. "Don, uh, can I ask you something?"

"Sure, anything."

"Well, um, how often do you and Mary still do it?" He asked uncomfortably.

Don took a sip of water and looked over at James thoughtfully. "I dunno, maybe three or four times a month... ah, more in the summer time I think. Why? What about you and Alice?"

James looked out to sea, and sighed inwardly. He desperately wanted to talk about the state of his marriage to someone, but had reservations common to many men about how intimate such conversations should be between friends.

"Alice and I have had sex twice in the last four years… and before that, it was about an average of a few times a year."

"Jeez man, how do you cope with that?" Don half turned on the seat so he could look at his friend, searching to see if in fact this might be a friend in need of a deep and meaningful conversation. As a volunteer counsellor with Lifeline, he liked to think he could be there for others when they needed him, but had not seen this kind of conversation starter coming from his friend. He quickly checked his memory banks to see if he could identify his perceptions about the state of James's and Alice's relationship, but found that nothing came to mind in terms of noting affection between the two, but neither had any sense of there being anything wrong.

James took another sip of water and kept staring out to sea. "Well for a start I moved into my own room about eight months ago, and well, you know, you just cope I guess…" A subtle flick of the wrist made it clear to Don that James was referring to masturbation.

Don put his hand on James's shoulder in a gesture of caring. "Man that's tough… but what about affection, intimacy. Don't you crave someone to touch you sometimes?"

In answer, James looked down and breathed deeply. Fighting back a lump of emotion that suddenly made it difficult to speak, he considered the enormity of the question, and realised that yes, he was actually starving for affection, but had not until that moment thought about just how much. Don's hand, still on his shoulder lay there like a very welcome dead weight on him, and he prayed for a moment that he would leave it there for a bit longer. It was, the only time anyone had touched him at all, apart from business handshakes, in nearly a year.

As the silence lingered, Don wondered what to say next. Questions flooded his mind, and raged battle for prominence before he settled on asking: "So are there physical reasons for this or are you two just fading out of each other's lives somehow?"

James turned to look at Don, and calmly replied, "No, just that after nearly fifteen years of asking and mostly being turned down, I stopped asking after a while. And then it got too hard to ask, and so now we're at the end... end of the road with it. Alice used to like sex back in the early days, but it seemed to become a chore or something after a few years, and then it became a weapon she'd use for either getting what she wanted, or punishing me for misdemeanours." He laughed, but there was no humour in it. "In fact, she managed to work out precisely what she could do to get exactly what she wanted so easily, I'm almost embarrassed to admit it. I'm not prepared to believe all women are like that, but Christ it's been a helluva lesson in a woman's ability to manipulate a man. Well this man anyway."

He turned and looked out to sea again, and Don removed his hand and did the same. As both men focused outwardly on the scene before them, each struggled with the thoughts invading their minds about the other. Finally Don spoke. "Have you thought about your options?"

"You mean like having an affair?"

"Well that, or even or leaving. But don't you think some counselling might help before you do anything drastic? I mean, do you love Alice?" Don queried.

James took a long moment to consider his reply. "Alice refuses to have counselling, and I'm not sure that leaving is a great option, because it would be expensive. I can't say I'm still in love with her, because I'm really not, and yet, I do feel we've got twenty years of history and that maybe we shouldn't just throw it away. Yet, I really don't think I can go on like this. Neither of us are happy, and I'm increasingly being made to feel like I'm only useful for bringing in the money. I don't think she's having an affair with anyone either, and I am sure that if I was caught in such a situation there would be absolute hell to pay... so I've not ever gone down that track as tempting as it might be at times. I really don't know what to do, but talking to you today has helped. Thank you." He patted his friend on the back, and stood up. "Come on, enough of this sad sack stuff, let's go to Bunnings."

Don looked up at James and grinned. "Hey you're welcome anytime buddy. Take it easy though ok, and don't do anything rash."

Later that evening, as James was lying in bed, searching his iPad for some porn, he thought about their conversation again, and wondered whether Don and Mary were in fact still in love, or 'just married' but with a better understanding of each other and therefore a better relationship overall. Did love last? He decided to turn the light out and simply ponder the question.

CHAPTER 2

Alice tapped her foot impatiently and smoothed her hair back before crossing her arms and hugging herself. For goodness sake, where was James? If there was one thing she simply could not abide, it was tardiness, and most especially when it was her husband being the tardy one. They were due to go out to dinner in only thirty minutes to celebrate her birthday, and she jolly well expected better than to have to wait for him.

As she watched out the kitchen window, Don and Mary drove up their driveway and parked in front of their garage doors. They both got out and started up the stairs to their front door before Mary broke away and went over to look at something in the garden. Don followed her and put his arm around her pulling her close as he too bent to investigate. She then picked a flower and handed it to him, which he promptly tickled her under the chin with. Mary smiled before leaning in to kiss him gently. It was a kiss that was comfortable and tender, and spoke of love between too old lovers who still felt passion for each other…the kiss not too long and not too brief.

Alice frowned. She didn't particularly like Mary, finding her carefree attitude about most things at odds with her own finesse. Mary was apparently happy to have a messy kitchen, where she cooked the most beautiful meals, and was always baking treats. When they all moved into their houses within two weeks of each other, Mary would often pop over with a dessert or a batch of cookies she'd made, but eventually stopped doing it when nothing was reciprocated and it took Alice a long time to return her dishes. Mary hung her washing out in a slap dash way, compared to Alice's clothes always lined up just so, and colour matching the pegs perfectly. Mary's other sins according to Alice centred around playing loud music with the doors open to their deck and pool area, and frequently holding noisy dinner gatherings and pool parties. Overall, she considered Mary to be quite loose with her attitudes to most things, and although James and Don got on well, she much preferred to have her own company than to put up with Mary on a regular basis and so refrained quite pointedly from encouraging a friendship.

As far as friendships went, Alice really felt that they were a waste of time in general. She had a couple of friends whom she'd known since high school, and they'd get together every year or so for a bit of a catch up, but they were not really confidantes. They'd compare husbands, trips taken, purchases made, and future travel or renovation plans, but after a few hours, there was often little left to talk about. Cards were sent at Christmas, gifts sent when an engagement, birth, or family event took place but one could hardly call them all close friends by most peoples' standards.

The truth was, Alice felt that most people were somewhat undeserving of her company. At least that's what she told herself. She'd been a very pretty young girl, and as such somewhat spoiled by her parents who had high hopes of her marrying well. She had certainly done that, but soon found that being married to a doctor had its challenges. He was never home, barely cared about what was cooked for him, and never noticed the state of the house she'd spent most of her time keeping clean and orderly. When Deanna was born, things got worse as she found him to be totally inept at helping with her parenting duties and tired as she was from doing everything, the lack of support from her husband drove her to despise him. Within three years of their wedding day, she developed a deep suspicion that he was having an affair and grew shrewish in her judgement of him and how he spent his time.

Finally confronting him one day, she found that she'd cornered a bear who was not only stubbornly uninterested in her theories of how he was spending his time and at what cost that was to her and their daughter, but that the more she pushed him to respond, the angrier he became until he finally pushed her away, causing her to bang her head on the light switch on the wall.   As she felt the crack, and found that her head was indeed bleeding, he further infuriated her by walking away and leaving her there.

Taking herself to the emergency department by taxi, she managed to get her moderate head-wound fixed up and decided to lay a complaint about her husband for having shoved her and causing the accident.

Before long there was a police officer questioning her, and advising her to consider her own and her child's safety, and then a senior member of the hospital staff was asking if she was alright? Further inspired by the way she was treated at the hospital, within two days she had had the locks changed and   his bags were on the doorstep.

Her insistence that he was a violent abuser led to a particularly nasty divorce and his subsequent decision to move to another city. He turned his back completely on her and Deanna, swearing to have nothing to do either of them save sending the monthly child support cheque, which he worked hard to have reduced to a minimum amount.

Now many years later, she was thinking about those days with her ex husband again as she wondered where James was and why he was becoming increasingly unreliable these last few months.

Men were so easy to manipulate, she thought, but when you really wanted them to step up and 'be a man' they were ridiculously weak and ineffective. James thought she didn't know much about him, or his business, or his friends, but she maintained a careful eye on his activities at all times. She knew the passwords to his email account and his phone, and regularly checked up to see what he was doing. When she wanted him to buy her something pretty and expensive, she always checked on his account balances in his business accounts to be sure there were no excuses for getting what she wanted, and laughed quietly to herself as she realised he had never noticed that she was also checking his diary.

Oh, where was he! Mary and Don had made their way inside and darkness was setting in for the night. Street lamps popped on so suddenly that she blinked to see if she'd imagined they were not in fact on moments before. Finally, she heard the Mustang round the corner and come into view.

Alice didn't care about the car – at least while James was happy with that ridiculous vehicle, he was busy and still willing to leave her alone. She didn't drive herself, and didn't really care how she was transported so long as it wasn't by bus or train, but did find herself a little jealous at times over the endless attention he paid to the vehicle. It was just a car for goodness sake!

As she looked below, Brett and James got out of the car, chuckling at some joke she was sure to hear about later. Brett was a blessing. He'd moved in just a few years ago, and seemed to breathe fresh air into the house. He was funny, liked her, but didn't flirt, and he gave James someone to hang out with – further meaning that he didn't need to bother her with boring trivia or needy affection. Although in reality he'd stopped trying to convince her to do anything other than occasionally hold her hand for a couple of years now. She tolerated the hand holding and the rare touch on her shoulder or back because she was sure that it just wasn't worth arguing about. But she didn't really see the need for it.

Turning from the window, she glared at James as they walked in the room, before smiling a welcome at Brett. "Where have you been, we're supposed to be there in thirty minutes? You both need to change and we still have a ten minute drive. You know I hate being late!"

"I'll just have a quick shower then, it won't matter if we're a few minutes late you know Alice."

"You don't have time for a shower, just have a quick wash, and let's go. I don't see why I should suffer being late for my own birthday dinner just because you were late home from God only knows where." She picked up her purse and made ready to walk down to the car, ignoring his protest. She proceeded to the car while James disappeared into the bathroom, turning on the shower as he locked the door behind him.

Neither noticed Brett rolling his eyes and quietly exiting the room.

Forty-five minutes later they were seated at the Sails Restaurant overlooking the harbour, waiting on Deanna and Maddie to arrive. Alice was still upset about their being late, but had decided to stop speaking about it. That meant that everyone in the room could hear the silence in her face. For Alice, the silent treatment was a weapon to be wielded like a sword. The recipient of such treatment would most assuredly know that it was he or she at fault, and why. If an apology was not forthcoming, the silence would continue for as many days as it took for them to give in and accept responsibility for the problem. James, Deanna and even Brett had all learned that it was best to grovel an apology sooner rather than later.

Fortunately, this evening being a birthday dinner, for Alice, meant that all of the appropriate apologies for their respective lateness could be presented with their gifts. A silk scarf from Maddie, a bottle of Coco Chanel from Deanna, Gold Class Movie Tickets from Brett, and from James a delicate gold bracelet studded with diamonds, and two first class tickets to a cruise on the Diamond Princess.

Summer 2007

CHAPTER 3

Brett looked at his new best friend and business partner and smiled. "Yes, I think this is a great idea and I'm really happy for you. Don't worry it will work out fine." He stepped out onto the balcony and breathed deeply. "Oh – what a *gorgeous* view from this balcony... I almost hope this cruise does help to restore your marriage because then *I'll* move in here and leave you to it!"

James smiled and looked around at the apartment once more. Yes this definitely felt like a fantastic decision and there was big part of him that could not wait to live here. Having decided several months earlier to make a last ditch effort to save his marriage or leave, the final pieces of the puzzle were finally in place. Next week he and Alice were leaving for a ten day Pacific Cruise aboard the Diamond Princess, and he hoped that it might be an opportunity to reignite some romance between them. He'd gone all out and paid for an executive suite, with only one bedroom, and arranged for flowers to be delivered to their room on arrival, with champagne. He had even bought his wife a beautiful set of Victoria Secret bedroom wear that he hoped might send the very clear message he wanted to get things restarted between them.

Brett was only a little envious, but more of the holiday plans than anything else. After having recently broken up with his own partner Mike, he knew the challenges James was faced with. James valued him for his sales skills and within months had invited him to become a partner in his Property Consulting Business. Brett quickly took to it and was soon finding brilliant apartments to do up and flip for them; profitability was up by 30% for the year. James also really liked Brett, and despite or maybe even because one of them was gay and the other straight, they found in each other a brotherly love that each had lacked. Brett had moved into the granny flat on the large property that James shared with Alice and his friendship extended to her easily too. They were like a family, but Brett's first loyalty was to James for having given him the opportunity to pick himself up from the financial and emotional ruins of the breakup with his former partner.

It had become their habit to take business trips together to attend conferences and training programs to maximise their business model, and during these times away, started to talk to each other about everything going on in their respective lives. Brett realised that James was in a very difficult marriage, and yet still found he had a deep caring friendship with Alice. This made it difficult at times to be with them both, but so far they'd muddled through. James tried to make it easy by keeping out of the way at home when Brett and Alice were playing about in the kitchen with new recipes and socially they all retreated pretty much to their own corners of the house in the evenings. Still, Brett could see that the strain was taking a toll on his friend, and when this apartment came up, suggested that James should consider taking it over for himself and making some plans for his own future. He also felt that if that was not going to happen, he himself would take the apartment and cease living onsite with the dysfunctional couple.

They were just walking down to the car when James's phone rang.

"Hello." Brett picked up immediately that something was wrong. Then he heard James ask, "Which hospital?" Followed quickly by... "Yes I'm on my way..."

Brett waited for the explanation to come and didn't realise he'd been holding his breath.

"Alice has been taken to hospital with bleeding... that's all I know. Do you want me to drop you somewhere or would you come with me?"

"Of course I'll come with you. "James was already out of the carpark, and not really listening. They rode in silence, each lost in their own thoughts about what this might mean. On arrival at the emergency department, they were shown into the curtained area where Alice was being examined by a doctor who looked remarkably like Albert Einstein. He wrote something in his notes, turned to the men, and immediately identified James as being the probable husband.

"Mrs Strong has been menstruating for three weeks now apparently, and growing quite weak. So I'd like to have her admitted for some tests. Let's find out exactly what's going on... she's quite comfortable for the moment, but I've also given her something to help her sleep. Don't stay too long. We'll talk again after these first tests are in this afternoon. Please make sure you give your mobile phone number to the nurse."

With that he turned and left, leaving both James and Brett stunned into silence.

Autumn 2008

CHAPTER 4

Deanna decided to try a different tack. "Mum, for God's sake, you might be sick, but you're not dying right now either. Seriously, why don't you at least create a bucket list and get busy ticking off a few boxes. You and James were going on a cruise remember? You could still do that."

She looked at her mother in frustration, wondering why it was that Alice would not make an effort to live every day like it was her last when clearly she should have had the ability to do so. Grabbing the tray, she stomped out of the room. Reaching the kitchen where Brett was peeling potatoes in preparation for dinner, she poured the plates into the sink and ran the hot water.

It was plain to Brett that she was upset, yet again, and he cautiously ventured forth the question: "Are you ok?"

"Oh, she makes me so mad. I mean what a waste. And she is so bloody demanding. I don't know how James copes. She's not sick enough to be in bed all the time, but refuses to get up and do anything. I never thought of her as being a hypochondriac before but I'm going to reassess my view on that. "

"Yes she is hard work isn't she. I didn't really want to say anything before but have you noticed that even when other people are around, that she is quite demanding of James's time?"

"Yes, I thought so too."

"Well it's kind of affecting the business unfortunately, and I'm not quite sure what to do about it. Do you have any ideas?"

"Do you want me to talk to her? Or to him?"

"I'm not sure which, or even *if*, either would make a lot of difference. But it is a problem in some ways."

"What's a problem?" James had come into the kitchen and reached into the fridge for a bottle of water. "Hmm?"

Brett and Deanna exchanged a look that James quickly interpreted incorrectly. "Are you both unhappy about something to do with Alice or is it me? Come on spill!" He took a long sip from his bottle and glared at them both.

Brett spoke first. "Deanna was just talking about how frustrating it is that Alice is so unwilling to do anything but lie about and feel sorry for herself, but that she's also so demanding of everyone's time. I just added that I am concerned about the amount of time she's pulling you away from our business and…"

"And we were both wondering what to do about that." Deanna finished for him. "It's true, we are concerned, for both of you."

James drained the water bottle and sighed deeply before turning to look out the window. "I don't know what to do. At first we were all told that she had only a few months to live, and so we've worked on that assumption. Even though she keeps improving, surely the prognosis is much better now, it's an indefinite trap isn't it?" He turned and looked carefully at Deanna checking for any signs of her reading too much into what he'd just said.

When he had months ago been ready to leave Alice, the diagnosis of terminal cancer had been handed down, forcing them to cancel their travel plans, and James to reassess his decision to stay and see out the end game with his wife. After all, she had seemed to need him so much then and started to cling to him. The sense of being needed had a profound effect on him, and he drew closer to her than he'd felt in several years. She in turn slowly turned a corner and improved in her health remarkably. Now – she seemed almost back to normal, but having spent so many months in bed, had aged considerably and lost a lot of muscle tone. It was already difficult for her to move about the house without a walker, and yet her mind was fit, and her ability to be harsh, even cruel in her demands on them all, but especially him, was taking its toll.

Deanna walked over to him and put a comforting hand on his shoulder. "Would you like me to have a talk with her?" He was grateful to her for not picking up how he was really feeling, and for being so supportive and helpful. He knew he'd not have been able to get through these last few months without her and Brett.

"Yes please… if you think it might help."

Deanna ran a hand through her hair and leaving the kitchen paused in the hallway to view herself in the mirror hanging there. "Ok old girl, I think it's time we did a bit of battle," she said to her reflection and pulled a face!

"Mum, I want to talk with you about something." Sitting on the side of her mother's bed Deanna picked up her slender hand, and held it gently, looking into the older woman's eyes, she tried not to see the wrinkles that had grown deeper, and the pale colour in her cheeks. The eyes were still the same pale green they'd always been, and the set of her brows over them still arrested her thinking so easily. Deanna both hated and loved to upset her mother. Having been just the two of them for so many years, when teenage hormones hit her at the age of fifteen, she rebelled against every teacher, friend, and most of all her parents. Her absent father was called, railed at, cried over, and then sworn at for being a selfish bastard. Then her mother was held to account for every wrong doing, and every lost opportunity she'd experienced in life so far.

The two of them never fully recovered from those two tumultuous years of Deanna's discovery of sex, drugs, and rock bands. Boys who played guitar were like candy to her, and she indulged in every whim she could sexually and did a fair amount of experimentation with alcohol, pills, and weed. Dropping out of school she spent more of her 16th year working out how to most easily punish her mother and step-father for anything at all. Finally she was brought home by the police, stoned and half naked, having been arrested for stripping in the centre of town at 2am, in front of a visiting sports team.

She settled down a little as she got older. Becoming pregnant with Maddie at 17 stabilised her a little, but not for long. Even now liked to go out and party for entire weekends at a time and was a keen starter for music festivals that regularly rolled around, dragging Maddie with her whenever she couldn't persuade James and her mother to keep her for a while. For five years she'd held down a job in a call centre and was supervisor and trainer for four days a week, and loved it. It still gave her the time off to party on weekends, and paid well enough to satisfy her basic financial needs. James was always good for a handout if she needed more though and she made regular use of his kind generosity.

"Mum, I think you need to do something about James."

Sharp green eyes hardened and the brows raised a little higher. Inwardly Deanna shuddered at the thought of what might be about to come from this conversation and decided to tread lightly.

"What's wrong with James?" Alice's tone left no doubt that she already thought the worst. She withdrew her hand and sat up a little straighter, adjusting her pillow against her shoulders.

"Well I think he's quite stressed, and very upset about how you are, and how to help you keep getting better. This has been very hard on him and I think Brett is also concerned that the business is suffering due to James not being there a lot. So – I was wondering, perhaps we could find a way to make it easier for him to return to work properly and we can get you a day nurse maybe a few days a week, to cover when I can't be here and Brett and James need to work."

Alice looked at her daughter, searching for any sign of manipulation in her words. So James was suffering was he, oh poor man. And Brett was worried... how dreadful. Well they didn't have a death threat hanging over their heads did they? They could come and go as they all pleased couldn't they?Including Little-Miss-High-and-Mighty here.

As she closed her eyes and took a deep breath before speaking, Deanna had an incredible sense of being in the presence of a crocodile, with eyes that bore into her before retreating behind closed lids. But the moment was fleeting and Deanna was looking into soft green eyes again that now held some traces of remorse and care. And yet she still felt uncomfortable. "Darling, please send James and Brett in to see me for a chat won't you? Actually no, just James please. I'm sure we can find some way to help him to feel better about what I'm going through."

Deanna started to smile, and then her mother's words fully clarified inside her mind. Was Alice going to be helpful and supportive, or was she in fact about to drop Deanna into a muddy mire of deception and angst?

"Mum, please don't be so hard on James ok? He's really struggling with what's going on for you. He does love you, you know."

The fleeting crocodile image flashed back in her mind as Alice patted her hand and said, "Yes I know he does dear."

Spring 2008

CHAPTER 5

James knew it was wrong, and he broke out into a cold sweat several times as he drove towards the beach resort town of Noosa. The thought of what might happen if he was caught was still not quite enough to make him turn back and so he floored the gas pedal and overtook a line of cars straggling behind a truck.

Pulling into the Sheraton hotel, he glanced around nervously, hoping that he was far away from home enough to not run into anyone he knew, and headed inside to register. The concierge offered to take his overnight bag, but he declined the offer with a smile. "No thanks mate, it's only a light bag."

He stepped out onto the deck of the hotel room a few minutes later, and gazed longingly at the sea, before sending a quick text. 'Room number 510'. Slowly he started to relax and decided to take a cold shower. It was only a little after 2 pm; the sun was streaming down, the humidity factor up around 80%. Taking a little time to soap up and calm down, the anticipation of the evening ahead caused his cock to throb and he grabbed it and held it... savouring the feeling, wondering what it would be like to feel her warm mouth around it... he closed his eyes.

A little while later he paused for a moment to give thanks for the opportunity to be primed and ready for Kate to arrive, and that despite his sex life being a zero for more than five years now, that he still had the urge and the ability to perform sexually.

He had always enjoyed sex. Before meeting Alice, he had travelled the world, experienced life, and partied hard. Then, he had seen her at an open home he was looking through. She'd been there with her daughter, considering buying the small apartment, and he was there checking it out for a colleague who was into flipping properties for quick gain. Before she left, he'd struck up a conversation, promising that he knew of another place nearby that was similar but slightly better and more affordable. He gave her his card to verify his credentials as an agent and she handed over her number. She called him the next day.

What started out as a whirlwind romance progressed quickly to marriage, and for the first few years he thought they were both very happy. There were some things that rankled a bit, like her refusal to work, and her passion for spending money on frivolities he didn't really understand her need for. She liked to think they were wealthy enough to enjoy a first class lifestyle all the way, and was quite unrealistic about any mention he made about budgeting, and limiting the number of holidays they could afford. She was delighted with the house they purchased when they first married, and zealously regarded it as hers and hers alone. Decorating it to her own tastes, and filling it with a lot of what he simply referred to as clutter and junk. Slowly, he got used to her ways, and compensated with his own displeasure and frustration by the self-assurance he had that she loved him, and that she was willing to show him her love in a myriad of ways. He thought she was kind to the poor, something he was very passionate about, and donated regularly to the Salvation Army.

He believed her to be good to his friends, and was sure they all liked her too.

Slowly the cracks began to appear. By the time they moved to Australia he had noticed that she was increasingly unhappy with just about everyone and everything. She had little interest in his activities so long as there was always plenty of money to spend and trips to be planned. Her pleasure in their new home was marred by the fact that in her view it was a little too small, facing the wrong way just a little bit, the view was not quite so good, the pool was in the wrong place on the block and the bathrooms were not quite... well everything was just a little off. If they argued about anything, he was always in the wrong, regardless of who was actually right. Sex became a bargaining chip, her daughter was challenging, and her moods were increasingly extreme.

Now, for the first time in years, James was feeling a surge of excitement about being with a woman, and yet nervous as hell about it too. He changed his shirt for the third time, and convincing himself yet again that he looked just fine, when she knocked.

When he opened the door, he felt like the ground needed to open up and swallow him. There she was, beautiful, and smiling. And he couldn't move! Frozen to the spot, as the full reality of what they were about to do slammed him in the guts, until finally he forced himself to step back and allow her access to the room.

"What's the matter James, aren't you pleased to see me? Oh that view looks amazing! Well, here we are..." in under ten seconds Kate had staked her presence in the room, checked out the view, put her bags on the floor beside the bed and was standing beside the balcony with her hands on hips looking at him expectantly.

Recovering his composure, James walked over to her and smiled. Only a few inches separated them and still he hesitated. The smell of her fragrance, the billowing organza curtain behind her framing her face in white, and he longed to kiss her until the end of time. And still he hesitated. In the space of a second, he remembered why they were there, what had brought them to this moment. And then she reached up and cupped his face in hers and kissed him ever so softly on the lips.

An explosion in his mind took over and everything else disappeared except his desperate need to be inside her. As they deepened the kiss, he grabbed her hips and pulled her hard into him, grinding, kissing, and desperately trying to feel every part of her. She responded in kind, and they soon fell onto the bed as he dropped his pants and took his cock in his hand seeking for the place to home it. She suddenly backed away and tried to sit up, as he followed her across the bed not understanding. "Wait, I need to ... there, that's it," she gasped pulling her skirt out from between her legs where it had tangled. He barely noted that she was wearing no underwear, and pulled her back towards him, plunging into her silky depths.

Within two minutes it was over and he rolled off her, keeping an arm under her shoulders. Facing her he smiled, and simply said: "Hi there."

She smiled back. "Hey you."

"Sorry, I was a little impatient really, I... I just so desperately needed you. Are you ok? I mean, was that ok... um."

"Darling that was fine. And I'm sure when you are ready and we go again, it will be much more about it being my turn ok. But for now, no complaints ok?"

He smiled again, and kissed her briefly on the lips. "Oh my God you are so beautiful. I'm so glad you are here. I was a little nervous this morning... well actually a lot nervous. But now you're here and I can't even remember why I was."

She kissed him and got up to go to the bathroom. They lay on the bed and talked for the next few hours, intermittently making love slowly, starting, stopping, and finally at nearly six o'clock they wandered downstairs for dinner.

As they entered the restaurant, he cast about once more for any familiar faces, and finding none, asked to be seated out on the deck, in a quiet corner.

"So I guess I should ask, how is Alice?" Kate searched his face for any sign of conflict in his answer, and simply nodded when he said, "The same".

She had been aware of the circumstances of his marriage for several months now, being a volunteer at the hospital where Kate had been admitted a few months ago. She had seen him coming and going as a visitor and a chance to talk to him about what he was going through eventually arose. Her job was to ensure that the families of cancer patients knew what options they had for home care and if needed, financial assistance. After several conversations she developed a deep attraction to James, but took her time and waited until Alice was returned home again and resting comfortably.

Keeping in touch with James was easy as part of her work responsibilities, but soon coffee meetings were becoming lunches, and they both knew that there was potential for a lot more. James had confessed his intentions to have left his wife just prior to her diagnoses, and having been told that Alice had maybe only a few months to live, had agreed to stay with her until the end. But that had been nearly a year ago, and her health was improving quite steadily.

That improvement however did not extend to any change of attitude towards her existence. Instead, more than ever Alice liked to lie about and take up everyone's time by insisting on company for her every waking moment, mostly from the confines of her bedroom. Even the doctors had said that she needed to get up and about a lot more to maintain maximum activity so that she could continue to improve. She refused.

The more that time went on, the more demanding and selfish she became, and was a developing mean streak which for those close to her was at times astounding. Kate had heard a lot about this too, and sympathised with James enormously on matters such as this. From her work experience, she had noticed that some patients became this way toward the very end of their lives, whereas others became sweeter and more loving to their family and friends.

She put her hand out to hold James's as he continued to talk about what life was like at home. He withdrew it suddenly as though burned. "Sorry, I just… well holding hands in public would put me in a very difficult position if we were spotted by anyone who knows me or Alice."

"Seriously – we're here in a restaurant on a Saturday evening, we've been screwing our brains out all afternoon, and you're worried about being seen holding hands?" Kate felt suddenly very cross with him. "Perhaps we should have just ordered room service then." She stood up and collected her purse. "I'm going to the bathroom."

James watched her go, and sighed. "Well, I suppose I deserved that!" he said to himself quietly.

Early Summer 2008

CHAPTER 6

Alice plucked at the bedspread and frowned. This was becoming so tiresome! She watched James as he entered the room and bent down to lift her up from the bed. She could walk, but quite enjoyed it when he had to carry her downstairs. The wheelchair was a bit of an insult she decided, but then it did save her from having to tire so easily, and having James push her about meant that she always knew exactly where he was.

The taxi van was waiting patiently in the driveway, lights still on although it was clearly daylight now despite the early hour. Once inside and they were on their way, James finally acknowledged her properly for the first time that day. "Did you sleep well?"

"No – not really. I was too hot. Really you must get that air conditioning unit seen to James." She stopped herself from launching into her regular tirade about the air conditioner, and looked out the window instead. It was several weeks since she'd been out and the seasonal changes were apparent. It would not do to start this trip off on wrong foot she decided as she marvelled at the beautiful flame trees fiercely bright in the early sunlight. No, it was not as if she wasn't going to need him a lot more for the next ten days. Best to play it cool for a while at least.

She turned to him and smiled. "So here we are, finally off on our cruise after all this time. I do hope we both have a good time darling." She patted his hand briefly then returned her gaze to the scenes passing by outside. People running and walking dogs, cars starting their commute to work. She was so delighted to not have to be part of all that. No – stopping at home and watching television was far more interesting. And now having had an excuse to do not much more than that for more than a year now, she was increasingly happy with her lot. Not that anyone would know it.

She found that being waited on hand and foot was in fact a wonderful way to live. No responsibilities, never having to go near a supermarket again, and thank goodness, never having to attend dinners with people she didn't like anyway. No reason to let on ever that she was not really as sick as she knew everyone thought she was. It suited her perfectly well to while away her time this way.

Of course the one difficult area was James and ensuring he kept on believing she was dying, soon. For as long as she had his sympathy, she knew that this could continue. It certainly helped that every time she allowed herself to do so, she could easily get very ill, and almost as easily regroup and recover. Her doctors were really quite astonished. She put her ability to play this game down to the power of the mind, and what she'd been learning about that over the years. She had learned how to slip to the brink of her current prognosis and then rallied and before long been home from hospital again.

One thing she was sure of, if James knew what went on in her mind about him and her situation, he'd be long gone. Only a few months ago he had suddenly started acting very happy instead of dour and grumpy around her. Brett alerted her to the change of mood, and joked about how they must be falling in love again or something. She had also at that time been quite jovial. Brett's drawing the wrong conclusion sparked her own curiosity about her husband's mood lately and she observed him closely for a few days. There was definitely a fresh spark of something about him.

Late one night after everyone was asleep, she got up quietly and calmly went to his office downstairs and looked through his diary. There was nothing there that hinted clearly about anything going on, but she did notice he had a lot of lunch appointments with someone named K. She started looking for other mentions of 'K', and noticed that some of the entries were on weekends as well as weekdays, and that not all of his appointments were marked with only a letter – most in fact had the full names spelled out beside the time and date. *Mark Lewis, lunch… Nathan Bird, Starbucks*, or even *Lynda S, Sails Bar*. No there were very few other entries with only a letter to indicate who they were. Only 'K'.

She checked the bank accounts online – as she had always done – and found a few hotel receipts that didn't actually marry up with when he and Brett had gone away on business. "Mmmm, I wonder what you are up to you dirty old bastard?" she thought as she quietly made her way back to bed.

The next day she asked James to sit and talk for a while.

"Darling, I was worried about you a little while ago, you seemed so down and, well I know this is a difficult situation for both of us."

He looked at her carefully before answering. "Yes, it's been a long year hasn't it?"

Alice took his hand, and continued. "But you seem so much brighter these last few days. Has something happened?" She looked at him smiling, as though she was ready to pop champagne bottles.

"James, darling is everything alright?"

He withdrew his hand slowly and stood up. "Yes of course, I just had a few good wins at work this month that's all. In fact, I can afford to fly your sister over for a couple of weeks if you would like that?"

Alice smirked inwardly. 'Got ya!' she thought without shifting the smile from her face. 'If that's the way you want to play it, I can work with that.'

"Oh darling that would be wonderful. Yes I'd love to see Kay... I mean Katherine!" As she held his eyes arrested in hers for a moment, something withered and died inside him. 'She knows! Oh my God she knows.' He quickly left the room and went straight to the toilet and threw up.

Days later following on from several fits of temper at home over various things he had a mild heart attack. Alice smiled again when she heard the news. Yes, she'd got what she wanted, and James was going nowhere. Placed on a strict diet and stress free work plan, James was home a lot more, and she was able to start demanding even more of his attention. She was also sure that he'd dealt with the 'K' problem.

Now they were off on a cruise.

"Oh darling, look at the size of it. It's enormous." As the ship came into view, her excitement was genuine. The thought of being on a cruise ship for several days did actually appeal, she just wished that she could have maybe gone alone and made the most of her time there, albeit, it would be of course necessary to be catered to as an invalid. 'Oh well', she thought as the taxi came to a halt, 'at least I can have *everything* I want for the next few days.'

Summer 2009

CHAPTER 7

Brett was worried.   Worried about business, money, the itchy patch on his left hand, and most of all, he was worried about Alice, James, and Deanna, and what was going to happen to them next. From what he could see as the somewhat more impartial observer, Alice had James right where she wanted him and was using her illness to control all their lives.

It wasn't that he doubted her diagnosis and prognosis. After all, if the doctors said (again) that she had less than six months to live, then surely at some stage they were going to actually get that part right. No, despite the fact that they had been saying pretty much the same thing for near enough to two years now, and Alice was still going strong a lot of the time, he still did believe that she was very ill and most likely dying.

It was more that he wondered just how long James in particular would be able to keep going on the treadmill he was on, with the punishing routine of working and being totally at Alice's beck and call. He was still averaging about six hours a day at work, but that meant starting at 4 am, giving it three solid hours from his home office, breaking out for an hour or maybe two sometimes during the day, and then finishing up for an hour to two late at night. If Alice was awake, she expected James to be there keeping her company. Anyone could see that it was mind numbing for him. She did sleep a bit during the day, and was finally asleep by about eight each evening; that was when he and James were able to catch up and talk about what was going on outside the house.

Brett had committed to staying on in the granny flat downstairs for as long as James needed him there. They had become incredibly close friends, and as business partners they were outstanding too. Brett was also able to bolster his friend's spirits quite easily, most of the time, but lately, James had been heard talking to himself, and becoming forgetful. The days turned to weeks and then months with no end in sight. Brett supposed it would have been hard enough for two people who really loved each other, but he knew that James had stopped thinking of Alice as a wife and lover many years earlier, and if anything at all, really only saw her as a bossy older sister. But here they all were, stuck in this drudgery of a life with no real end in sight.

As he took another drag on his cigarette, Brett wondered what might happen if Alice did in fact continue to get better? At the moment she seemed to be in top spirits, and the doctors were once again trying to encourage her to get up and about more, even to take a holiday.

"There's no reason for you to be spending all your time in bed Mrs Strong," said Doctor Appana. "In fact, getting out and doing some moderate exercise would be good for you. How long since you swam in your pool? Or spent some time in your garden? Perhaps a stroll through the park – ok in your wheel chair if needed, but at least get some fresh sea air?" Doctor Appana had looked askance at all three of them standing at the end of the bed then, and when they seemed to avoid looking at her, she wondered why and held back from leaving the house until she got some answers.

Her beautiful dark pixie face clearly demonstrated her concern when Brett and James explained that no amount of coaxing ever seemed to get Alice to venture further than the living room sofa.

"But that's absurd!" she exclaimed, as she tucked a long strand of jet black hair back into a clip. "How long has this been going on? Most of my patients showing the amount of improvement your wife is would be desperate to get out and make the most of the life they have left in them. I don't understand at all!" She rummaged in her bag and produced a notebook. "I want you to start making a note of all the times that Alice leaves her bed each week, and please encourage her to at least get out to the garden. She would benefit from the vitamin D in the early morning sunshine at least, and when I see you in two weeks I want to know that she's been making an effort. I trust you both to help see that this happens."

"Look Doctor, I can see you are an intelligent woman. So I don't want to insult you at all, and I know you are doing your best, but quite simply, Alice refuses to be anything more than an invalid. Yes it's quite bizarre, and we're dealing with it. We've tried for years to get her *thinking* about a bucket list, let alone act on it, but she just doesn't want to." James sounded like a man with the weight of the world on his shoulders. The young doctor wasn't sure if she was looking at a grieving husband or just someone who was at the end of his tether with a wife who clearly had no desire to *live* for the rest of her life. The saddest part was, she could see that this could easily continue for at least another year, and had presumably sucked the life out of the other adults in the house over a long period of time already.

She shrugged gently and looked at each man before choosing her words very carefully.

"If Mrs Strong does not want to help herself, then you all need to consider what is healthy for each of you. Carers require a great deal of care themselves. I do hope you are all making the most of any opportunities to nurture your own health and wellbeing throughout this ordeal."

A quick rub of each man's arm in encouragement and she was gone. Brett turned to James who was staring out the window over the kitchen sink. "She has a point you know. We do need to look after our own needs too, especially you buddy."

A silent tear had escaped James's eye and was rolling unchecked down his cheek. It changed direction when it reached the line beside his mouth. Brett watched in momentary fascination. When had his friend's face become so aged? He turned away and left James to his window gazing, unsure whether to hug him or leave him to his grief. He reached his own room and opened a bottle of Jack Daniels, and spent the next few hours working slowly through it before falling asleep on the floor beside his bed.

Winter 2009

CHAPTER 8

Deanna finished wiping down the bench, put the plates away in the cupboard behind her, and contemplated throwing each one against the wall as she did so. Finally, she decided to just grab her umbrella and go for a walk. Stomping down the driveway, she was nearly collected by James and Brett in the Mustang, but chose to ignore them and marched off down the street.

Let them be pissed at her leaving Alice alone. Clearly it was not for very long – after all they'd just arrived home. If they weren't planning to stay, that was not her problem. At least not right now.

Alice had been difficult all morning, and managed to create ten times more work for everyone than usual. She had decided that she could no longer shower herself, and needed help with washing her hair and dressing, but Deanna was sure this was just another way of her manipulating and humiliating both her and James. She was, so far as Deanna was concerned, *perfectly* capable of performing her own bathroom care, and to assist, James had installed a wet room shower with a seat in the master bedroom ensuite recently. Sure, she might need a walker to get to the bathroom, and that was from her own damned laziness, but damned if she really needed *that* much help once she got there.

Deanna smiled as she recalled hearing James tell her mother that 'once you can't wipe your own bum Alice, it will be time to put you into full time care'. Alice had been furious, and they'd all laughed about it together downstairs later. Deanna had tried several times now to talk Alice into arranging for community nurses to come in and help her with her ablutions in the mornings, finding that she was really struggling to accommodate the need to both be there so often, and to take on this extra role of care.

Alice was having none of it. And yet, Deanna had seen evidence of her mother's ability to do much more for herself than she'd have them all believe only as recently as Saturday morning. Little things like finding Alice freshly dressed and combed first thing in the morning sometimes when clearly no one but she could have done that for herself. And things moved about in her drawers one day last week; clearly James would have drawn the line at rearranging and folding things so neatly, and re-organising a section of her wardrobe, but clearly these had been done. Which left the question burning in her mind, was her mother doing things in the night to keep herself active and busy but putting on a big act of helplessness during the day? But if so, why on earth was she doing that?

Deanna turned the corner and walked to a place in the park, found a dry bench to sit on and lit up a smoke. Replaying the day over in her mind, she further fumed at the way her mother had insisted on having the sheets changed for the second time in two days for no apparent reason. "The pillow cases smell funny, and they have to match the sheets..." "The windows are dirty and need cleaning – you know I like to see outside; can't stand smudges..." "This stew needed more salt, who cooked it? Go bring me the salt. Actually no I've decided I want a sandwich instead..." "These batteries are running out in the TV remote – go get me some more…"

It was relentless. And Deanna was so tired of it. What about *her* life. Why did it end up that she was tied to this place to care for an old bitch who didn't appreciate her anyway? Maybe she should just tell James and her mother that she had made plans to move away and do it. After all, now aged 16, Maddie was mostly staying at her boyfriend's anyway and clearly didn't need her to be a hands on mother any more. In fact there was really nothing keeping her here if she wanted to go. Stuff it! That would at least mean a change for everyone. In fact, to hell with it, she would do it. But where to go? And how would she be able to afford it?

The sad facts of her financial situation were as much of a challenge as her mother's demanding ways. She was terrible with money, and earned very little anyway. Four days a week she was at the call centre and while she didn't pay rent or board at home, between what she spent on smokes, taxis, and inconsequential stuff that she couldn't even name, not to mention what Maddie swiped from her wallet when she thought she could get away with it, she had barely $500 in the bank. She would have to plan this a bit better. Would James help her? If it meant making a change to the way they were all living, he might. But – he was looking like he was close to a nervous breakdown himself. God, how on earth did he stand it? Deanna could see quite clearly how much little love there was lost between her step-father and mother, but yet he was still here, and still doing everything he possibly could to make Alice's life comfortable.

Maybe it was just so many habits he had forgotten how to break. Saying yes, and giving in to Alice had become a bad habit, but how could any husband stand up to such a manipulative woman playing on all of them for sympathy.

A little while later, Deanna walked through the kitchen and interrupted Brett and James talking in quiet tones. The door through to the upstairs bedrooms was closed, and they were discussing Alice.

"Hi." James was the first to acknowledge her. Brett just nodded and wiped his eyes with a tissue.

"What's going on?"

Brett started to cry again. Sobbing quietly. "We're just talking about options, that's all. Pull up a chair would you like a cup of tea or something stronger?" James reached for a glass and put it on the table in front of the bottle of Jack Daniels that was by now half empty. Both had clearly had a couple of shots already in the last half hour.

"Thanks." Deanna poured herself a tipple and added a couple of cubes of ice from the freezer before sitting down.

James looked between the other two. "We all know I think that we can't keep doing this. It's just too hard. Alice is requiring more help, and I for one, was never cut out to be a nurse. Brett should not have to be helping to the levels he is – and I'm going to tell your mother that he is reserved for cooking dinners and ensuring there is food in the house etc, but that's all. No more having to sit with her and then running about after her whims. You," he looked at Deanna, "should not have to be sacrificing your own life at your age to deal with this either, and Alice is simply going to have to be told that starting tomorrow, a nurse will be here every day for two hours in the morning to get her started for the day, bathed, dressed, and made comfortable. That at the very least will give you and me a break from morning duties. If that works out alright I'll put the nurse on for the entire morning seven days a week so that we can all take a break and I for one can get back to work more often."

Brett took up his glass and gulped down the contents in one hit. "Yes I think that's a great idea, but she won't be happy." He shook his head firmly and his blonde curls flipped about his forehead.

"Well what do you think Dee?" He often called her that - she liked it.

Putting her glass down she tried not to show her tremendous relief over James's decision. "Well I think that's about the best news I've heard all year actually. But Brett's right, if she doesn't like the idea she will make our lives even more hellish than before."

James nodded. "Yes that's as may be, but, let's be realistic for a moment. Exactly what is she going to be able to do about it? She's bedridden, helpless, and despite her incredibly mean tongue, she can't do much more than badger us with words. I for one am not going to let her control me that way anymore."

Deanna looked at him suspiciously. "Ok, who are you and what have you done with James?"

Brett laughed. "Yes I agree with Dee, who are you really? This is a bit of a switch buddy."

James laughed with them both. "Well actually for the last two months I've been seeing a therapist. I had reached a point where I was sitting down the beach and looked up at the cliffs along on the point, and wondered what it would be like to jump off them and put an end to all this. Don and I have talked a bit about what's going on here, although not in any great detail, but when he suggested counselling I thought it might be a good idea. I'm sorry to admit this to you both but I finally realised I have at some level been thinking very seriously about ways of killing myself for a while.

Georgina has helped me to see that this is not worth my own life ending, but that I, we, all of us have the ability to take a lot more charge over this situation than we have been allowing. In fact, we've perhaps been allowing Alice to rule our lives very unfairly and it's time we, or at least I, stood up to her. She can't actually *do* anything to me at this point."

"Well she could …" Deanna stopped, unsure if it was fair to say it out loud.

"What, divorce me? Ha! Wouldn't that be bloody ironic?"

"No, but, well yes, or she could write us all out of her will?" Deanna took another sip of her drink and twirled the ice cubes around in the bottom of her glass. She looked uncertain, and Brett mirrored her expression.

James sighed. "Do you really thing that would be a problem? No the bigger challenge would be convincing every friend and acquaintance we have that I was not the bastard divorcing his dying wife. And we all know that is exactly how it would look. But really, does the idea of that feel worse than what we're doing now? I mean look at us. We're all trapped here by this woman who seems to despise us all, who never actually dies, despite doctors saying she's only got months to live for the last two years… For God's sake, this is ridiculous!" He laughed dryly. "Hell I think we're all at greater risk of dying than she is each time we cross the bloody road."

Their individual thoughts on that were interrupted by a banging on the floor upstairs. They all stood up together. "Um James, I think I should tell you something." The banging started again.

"Yes?"

Deanna looked uncomfortable "I think she gets up in the night and does stuff."

He frowned. "What do you mean 'Stuff'?"

"Well I think she potters about quite happily in her room sorting out drawers and things in her wardrobe. I, well I just think that's odd given how much she wants us all to think she's so incapable of anything. Don't you?"

"Yes that *is* a bit odd." The banging was now constant. "Later, ok?" And he went upstairs.

Hell Hath No Fury

Spring 2009

CHAPTER 9

Alice was incredibly angry. Where was it? Someone must have taken it. She can't possibly have simply lost it - that was ridiculous. The jewellery case in her hands shook as she tried to put it up high in the wardrobe. Damn, it was too high. Wait. Think carefully Alice, she said to herself. Find another place. If someone was stealing her jewellery then a new hiding place was needed anyway. She moved a couple of jumpers out of the way and put it behind them for now. Yes that was it. It would do anyway.

As she toddled back to bed, she wondered if she could still make do with her plan. Maybe. It wouldn't take much really. To get away from here. No, she would have to be careful though. And what about the doctors? Well, she could easily find doctors somewhere else. Yes, that would be ok. After all, they were all pretty bloody useless really.

She climbed back into bed and rubbed her eyes, willing the thoughts to come. Three months ago, she had been browbeaten and bullied into having to accept a day nurse in to care for her. That was the last straw she decided. For her family to treat her like that was just too much to bear. Didn't they know how sick she was? No, wait a minute, she'd had to reconcile that thought with the knowledge that she was in fact nowhere near as unwell as she'd have had them all believe. Was she overselling it? Even to herself?

She lay back on her pillows and thought about the big idea that had finally come late one night as she went through her jewellery box. She had money – lots of it. She had been filing away funds for more than twenty years waiting for the day she could leave her stupid husband. She'd had gifts of diamonds and gold - lots of them - from James over the years, and knew that these could help to fund her escape. She estimated there was at least $100,000 worth of jewellery, and another similar sum of cash sitting in her own bank account earning high interest. No one knew about that but her. When internet banking had been introduced about ten years earlier, she had learned quickly how to hide her nest egg, and simply plotted to use it one day. The gift of the iPad last Christmas had made the regular trek to James's office less necessary, and it was password protected of course.

She lay back and started working out what to do. And when? Timing was going to be critical. She was never alone anymore, thanks to that bloody nurse. But – Brett and James were going away to Asia in a few weeks for a conference, and her granddaughter Maddie had agreed to come and stay to help as Deanna was possibly attending a school reunion. Maybe she would be able to convince Maddie to get a few drinks under her belt and fall asleep. Well wouldn't everyone be very surprised to find her just 'gone'. Yes, that was almost worth staying for, to see the looks on their faces.

"Well officer, we don't really know how we lost her. Yes she is bedridden, and deathly ill, but she's no longer anywhere to be found. We even looked under the bed!" Alice smiled as she thought of it.

Serve them all right. And where would she be? On her way to some place. She still hadn't quite decided where yet.

She was spending every night walking about her room, ensuring she had enough strength to leave, which was exhausting her during the day, resulting in her sleeping a lot more... further enhancing her position as weak and dying.

Her plan was simply to leave, in the night, and taking only a change of clothes, her jewellery box, and her iPad, passport and wallet. She would book into a small hotel, then the next day make her way to the airport and buy a ticket.   To anywhere. Yes that was it, she'd simply go somewhere and just settle there.

She suddenly realised she'd forgotten the issue of getting her medical records.   One more trip into hospital might be needed. As she drifted off to sleep she tried to conjure up another way for that to happen, but her mind was tired and she couldn't quite hold the thoughts together.   "Damn this medication for making me fuzzy minded..." was her last thought for the night.

Early Summer 2009

CHAPTER 10

Maddie rolled her eyes at her grandmother, wondering how on earth she was actually going to get through the weekend without giving in to the desire to stuff a pillow over her head. She'd only been there for two hours and already Alice had made her feel like an abject failure in life.

"Your tattoos are just ugly my dear, and you used to have such pretty arms. Don't you want to look nice in a wedding dress one day? Well no one in their right minds will want to marry a girl with all that ugliness on their bodies would they? Although I suppose you'd much rather live in sin… how many boys dear? One, two as a time? Yes your mother was a bit of a slut too really. I tried to keep her clean and safe, but no, she just wanted to get drunk and party with boys… just like you seem to Maddie. Well you know you'll just end up like her too won't you. Yes, the boys will stop finding you so pretty and accommodating once you've got a baby too. Yes, stupid to have children my dear, best to wait. Don't you want to make something of your life one day? I suppose you think that working in a shop is a good job don't you. Well if you are holding out for me to die so you can get some money, don't you worry about that young lady. There won't be anything. I'd bet my life on it that James will keep it all and take up with some young slut the minute I've gone. He won't give you anything, and I'm still deciding about leaving everything to the cat shelter..."

She just went on and on... Maddie took the lunch tray and left the room without saying anything. She had arrived yesterday, and was supposed to stay until the end of the following day, if she could stand it for another minute.

Every time she walked in the room Alice would find something to criticise about her hair, clothes, make up, lack of a good job, her mother, her boyfriend... there was nothing off limits it seemed. Maddie was unsure about the memories she'd had of Alice from when she was a very young child, having always thought Gramma was very sweet. She'd spoil her with sweets, and brush her hair for what felt like hours each night before reading a story at bedtime. She had never really been affectionate, but she had made Maddie feel loved. When had that all changed? She pondered this as she stacked the lunch dishes, and then went outside for a smoke.

The day passed achingly slowly, with Maddie carefully avoiding spending too long at a time in the room with Alice, saying there was a lot to do in the kitchen to prepare for dinner. Not that Alice was able to eat much these days it seemed. Maddie wondered for the hundredth time what exactly was wrong with her grandmother having lost track of what it was really all about years ago. It felt like she'd been sick for years, and she knew that everyone made out that the old girl had cancer of some sort, and should have died already, but just kept on getting better enough to hold on and make all their lives miserable. Not that she really cared, so far as she was concerned, Gramma had turned into a spiteful old woman who just annoyed a lot of people now. Poor Grampa James.

The day stretched out and they even managed to get through a few hands of gin rummy before finally it was dinner time and Alice was ready to retire for the night. Maddie headed downstairs to drink and eat her way through the bottle of white wine and tub of mint chocolate ice-cream.

She was woken from where she'd fallen asleep in front of the TV in the family room much later by a thump, followed by a groan. "Oh Shit, the old girl's fallen out of bed has she!" Maddie turned the light on in the hallway and was about to turn and go upstairs when the nearly tripped over the body of her grandmother lying at the foot of the stairs.

"Oh shit, oh shit… fuck! What the… shit…" She turned another light on and bent over Alice checking to see if she was breathing. The options of Ambulance, Deanna, and James all jumbled in her mind as she grabbed her mobile from her pocket, and speed dialed her mother. The clock on her phone had already advised it was 2.25am. Deanna picked up the phone on the second ring.

"What is it? Y'ok?" she asked sleepily.

"Mum, I think Gramma's dead. Mum, I don't know what to do can you get here?"

"What? What do you mean she's dead? Where are you? Maddie, take a deep breath and calm down ok?"

Maddie took a couple of deep breaths, and started slowly. "Mum, I just woke up and heard a bump, and thought she'd fallen out of bed, so I was going up to see and I nearly fell over her lying at the bottom of the stairs. She never gets out of bed any more so I thought… hold on a minute."

"Maddie – is she breathing?"

"Yes, she is, but she's out cold. Should I call an ambulance?"

"Yes I think that's a good idea. I can do that for you if you like, and I'll call James. We can all get there by morning I'm sure. Not the ambulance, no that won't take long... ok I'm going to hang up and do that and call you back ok... ok?"

"Mum something's really weird."

"What do you mean?"

"Well for a start she's fully dressed, and there's a small bag half lying under her body."

"What? That's ridiculous... what?" Deanna was struggling to comprehend Maddie's words.

"She's dressed Mum, and even has shoes on. Like she was going out somewhere."

"You're fucking kidding me!"

Several hours later, Deanna and Maddie stood in the dining room with James and Brett surveying the contents of the bag Alice had presumably been trying to leave the house with. There was a pair of shoes, socks, two night gowns, two dresses, one of which was suitable for evening wear only, and her favourite cardigan. Her medication from the bathroom was there along with her toothbrush, paste, and mouthwash, and moisturiser. But the strangest items were the passport, outdated as it was, and a lot of her most expensive pieces of jewellery wrapped in a small hand towel. The only other thing of note was a small coin purse containing a VISA debit card and an ATM card – again, both outdated, but from a bank that James was unfamiliar with.

"Was she running away? I mean what the hell is this? I thought she was bedridden!" exclaimed James.

He was simmering with fury inside. Feeling duped, and stupid at the same time. "How could she have conned them all so well. Or had she? Was this the packed belongings of a woman who had really thought through the idea of escaping from home, or was it a serious sign of diminished mental capacity?" He wasn't sure but maybe it was a combination of both.

Clearly his wife, who had still not regained consciousness, had got up in the middle of the night, packed a small bag of belongings, dressed herself, despite having everyone believe she was barely able to even get out of bed alone, taken all her most expensive jewellery and then fallen down the stairs. She also had bank accounts presumably with another bank that he had been unaware of, and with all that jewellery in her possession perhaps some intention to sell it? "Where was she planning to go? There had been no taxi called. And it was at least a kilometre long walk to the nearest anything from their house."

Perplexed ever more as he looked at the items on the table, and still struggling to make sense of the entire situation, he sat down and looked up at the others. "So, you're all awfully quiet – what do *you* think she was doing?"

The sudden sound of the doorbell ringing interrupted whatever Deanna was about to say.

Moments later two police officers were introducing themselves and they all sat down at the table.

"We're not here to arrest anyone, don't worry. But we do need to follow up as a routine enquiry. It's fairly standard procedure in cases like this you understand." stated the first officer.

"Well officer, let me just clarify that assumption for you right now, there's nothing standard about this at all." snapped Deanna. She was also angry at her mother, not least because Alice had managed to spoil her first real weekend away for months, but also had raised so many questions with her bizarre behaviour – as evidenced by the items on the table.

"Would anyone like a cup of coffee?" Brett stood up and started to fill the kettle. Bustling about the kitchen, he took coffee orders from the officers, and kept everyone from talking with chatter about coffee plungers vs Nespresso machines. Finally they were all seated again, stirring sugars and milk into cups and eyeing each other nervously.

"Would you mind telling me what you mean by that comment about this being 'nothing standard'?" questioned the first officer again.

Officer Burrows, according to his name badge, flipped open his small note pad and warmed up an old Bic pen till the ink ran smoothly before writing the date and time at the top of the page.

The second policeman, whose badge read 'Officer Cork', just folded his arms and leaned back on his chair a little, assessing each of the four members of the household.

"Miss Strong?"

"Actually no, it's Ms Wood." Deanna looked up at James and smiled. "James and Mum have been married for donkeys' years, but I was not adopted. My daughter here is also Miss, er Ms Wood. Well what I meant was, that Mum has been bedridden for about two and a half years now. She was first diagnosed with cancer and given a fairly short term prognosis. She promptly took to her bed then and sort of never really gets out of it."

James cleared his throat and loudly slurped a mouthful of coffee. "Yes that's right officer. My wife seems to have taken an absurd delight in having us run after her constantly satisfying her every whim, while she got on with the business of dying. What none of us have been aware of these last few months was that she even had the ability to dress herself, let alone try and make run for it in the middle of the night. So you see we're all quite stunned to have found her not only lying fully dressed at the bottom of the stairs, but apparently planning to take off somewhere with a bag, full of expensive jewellery, and a couple of outdated credit cards from a bank I never knew she had accounts with."

His voice had risen at the end of his tirade, and the officers were left in no doubt at all that he was not only surprised but quite angry over his wife's behaviour.

"So you see gentlemen, we four are feeling a little put out by all this, and the three of us," he pointed to himself, Brett, and Deanna, "had arranged weeks ago to be away this weekend and for Maddie here to stay and look after Alice because she could not fend for herself or be left alone.   Suffice to say, we think we've all been conned somehow."

"Thank you Mr Strong, I appreciate the background information. Has your wife tried to do anything like this before?" questioned Burrows.

At this James visibly shook with anger and frustration.   Brett jumped in to save him having to answer. "Officer, for the last two years the only time Alice has ventured past the landing at the top of the stairs was when James was able to carry her down them.   Aside from coming into the lounge on those occasions, she has been to the hospital twice in the past twelve months for tests, and then back to bed upstairs.   We are not joking when we tell you this has been a helluva shock to us all."

"Officer Cork finally spoke: "Thank you, all of you. We can see you're upset. And you've been very helpful. Would you mind if we just take a quick look at the stairs and her bedroom before we go?"

"Help yourself."   Brett made to rise from the table, but the policeman waved him back down.

"It's alright – we'll just take a quick look and be on our way. Enjoy your coffees."

A few minutes later Officer Burrows came back into the room, made a quick note of each of their full names and dates of birth, and left with his partner.

Later that day Don and Mary came over to see if there was anything they could do to help. Mostly they wanted to know what was going on, but James was sympathetic to their curiosity.

"So what happens now?" Mary looked at James with one eyebrow raises and a smile on her face. He could see that there was definitely an amusing aspect to the story, but was unable to return the smile.

"Well, Alice apparently hit her head and has a concussion but no other apparent injuries. So she should be home tomorrow, and from there we'll be asking some hard questions I suppose."

Mary and Don looked at each other, both wondering if it was appropriate to ask the question they each felt was the biggest one of all – would James stay? Was this the end? Mary knew from conversations with Don that James had felt miserable but trapped for years now and yet neither could see how he was ever going to extricate himself from this drama. Today's events might change things considerably.

James observed the look that passed between them and cleared his throat. "I'm not sure what will happen long term but for now this might change things for the moment. Let's hope so."

As Mary and Don walked home a short while later holding hands, James watched after them with more than a touch of envy over their closeness and thought how 'normal' they seemed compared to himself and Alice.

Autumn 2010

CHAPTER 11

James was busy, grumpy, and aware that he was probably aging quite quickly with being constantly in those two states lately. Six months had passed since Alice tried to run away, and despite the fierce arguments that occurred in the weeks that followed, Alice remained tight lipped about her intentions that night maintaining she must have been sleep walking. Now, with barely four hours a day to get out of the house and focus on some business matters, he was constantly rushing, and that was making him short with everyone around him simply because it was just. too. much!

The demands of being married to a woman who barely let him out of her sight, and demanded his attention constantly was starting to affect him terribly. She was devious enough to have planned – albeit badly - to run away, and that she had apparently been hiding money and jewellery for years dumbfounded him. And yet here he was still in the position where he was unable to leave. Her attitude when she came round in hospital the following day was to deny everything. But he could see the glint in her eye, and cunning in her smile as she confessed her love for him.

He barely made it out of the room before erupting in anger that must have made the nurses walking past wonder what on earth was upsetting him, but he was clearly unapproachable in the moment and so they let him be. Brett came up to him a while later and James was able to share what she'd said about the previous night's incident, and his utter disbelief at her guile.

The stress of it all had him taking several forms of anti-stress medication, but he'd refused his doctor's offer of more counselling sessions knowing that would further cramp his ridiculous schedule. One thing he had been able to do was persuade her doctor to help him convince Alice that she needed to have some additional tests on her health status that included mental health checks. Not that Alice was really aware of the breadth of the testing – but both he and Dr Appana wanted to see what might be happening mentally as a result of her botched run away plans.

Head down and deep in thought he nearly didn't hear the voice behind him as he reached for his keys to unlock the car.

"James, is that you?"

He turned around and was startled to see an old friend standing beside him. "Petra?"

They both opened their mouths to speak and just smiled instead. Petra was first to speak. "I thought it was you. Goodness, it's been years, but you haven't changed a bit!"

Petra's eyes were bright, and her smile was wide. James couldn't remember how long it had been since he'd last looked into those warm brown eyes, but he remembered fully how he'd always felt about her. They'd been good friends many years ago, when they'd lived in the same apartment block, and Petra had struck up a friendship with his girlfriend at the time, Cheryl.

"What are you doing here? This is such a surprise. Wow, you look amazing!" With that James took a step forward and wrapped his arms around her in an enormous hug. Then realised he didn't want to let go – ever!

Petra helped by stepping back first and taking his hands in hers, held his arms wide as though to get a better look at him. "No, you have not changed one bit. Although I do think you've lightened up a bit and at least stopped wearing all those dark t-shirts and black jeans. Nice to see you in some colour for a change." She laughed and let go of his hands.

"Do you have time for a cup of coffee?" asked James, a note of uncertainty in his voice.

"No, I'm so sorry, I don't right this minute, much as I'd love to. I had to be somewhere about ten minutes ago. But here's my card, give me a call and let's catch up soon ok? Anytime. I'm living about twenty minutes up the highway, but happy to drive back down this way to meet up." And with that she had turned and left, calling over her shoulder that she expected to hear from him within a few days.

He watched her as she reached her VW Golf, put her shopping bag in the bag seat and with a quick flick of her straight dark hair disappeared into the driver's side. He wondered about what she'd been doing for the last dozen years or so since they'd last met over drinks and dinner. Then his mind went back further to the many times before that spent talking for hours, laughing over silly things. Her being her obnoxiously rude to him when he and Cheryl had split up, before deciding that her friendship was perhaps stronger with him than with Cheryl after all. They'd talked that one through too, and promised to always keep in touch.

Life had taken over though. She'd married some dickhead from up north, then he'd been married to Alice; she had divorced the dickhead, but then married her childhood sweetheart who later died, at about the same time as he'd moved with Alice to Australia.

Petra played on his mind for the entire drive home, and then as soon as he had a quiet moment to himself he went online and looked her up. Her status on Facebook was set as single. They still had some friends in common but he realised with a pang, that he'd also sadly allowed those friends to disappear into his own history books.

Later that night he called and arranged to have an early lunch on Friday, and then asked Brett to cover him at home saying he'd an urgent and very important meeting to attend. That gave him the morning to get through his work commitments, and an extra two hours for lunch.

The next two days dragged on and finally they were seated at a table talking about old times and new trends in their lives as though they'd seen each other only a week ago. She was a chatty sort of woman, and filled in an hour easily bringing him up to date with her work life, children's stories, and tales about her friends, moving to Surfers Paradise and plans for the next few months. Finally, it was her turn to ask about his life.

"So, how's Alice? You've not said much about her. In fact, I'd go so far as to say you've avoided talking about her, but you're still wearing your wedding ring - Is everything all right?"

Her directness reminded him of the many times she'd been that way in the past, almost as though she could see right through him and would not hesitate to call him on anything that seemed off to her. He looked at her for along moment and wondered how much he could get away with not saying. Then decided that subterfuge was pointless.

"I'm living in hell. Quite simply, I have no idea when this will end, but I've a hope that when this is finally over, I'm not too stressed and old to get to enjoy some quality time of my own." As he said the words he suddenly felt as though a balloon inside him had been punctured and deflated.

The story came pouring out then, with a few tears that he'd tried and failed to hold in. God it was so good to be able to talk to someone, anyone, but especially his old friend Petra, about the state of his marriage and his life. "So you see, she has cancer, and perhaps some form of mental health issues too, but while technically she's dying, she's been this way for several years now, and I'm more or less stuck. I was in a loveless marriage to start with, and was ready to end it when the diagnosis came, along with a prognosis of only a few months to live. Sadly, this has proven to be an extreme case, with her constantly surprising her doctors with remarkable resilience, but at home, she's just demanding, mean, and at times almost impossible to live with at all."

Petra handed him a serviette to wipe his eyes with and he took it gratefully. He noticed the waiter hovering quietly in the background and made a mental note to tip him well for having the courtesy to not interrupt what must have been an obviously difficult conversation.

"But what do you do to cope? I mean, surely you must be able to get out and do 'life' even if she doesn't want to. For God's sake, it's not like she has anything over you to keep you there, is there? I mean James, you are a strong, capable man, who is not the sort to take shit from anyone. How has she managed to play you into such a tight corner?"

James felt colour rush up his neck, and tugged at his shirt. She was right, but how to explain it to her. He didn't want to risk losing her respect, regardless of how well she knew him. He was sure she'd judge him harshly for not respecting himself. Floundering for an answer, he simply shrugged and picked up his glass of water.

She was looking at him like a bird eyeing up a big fat worm, clearly expecting some sort of answer. "James, seriously, what's going on?"

Drawing a deep breath, he found his voice, but was unable to meet her eyes for more than the briefest of moments. "She makes everyone's life difficult, and if I mess with her moods and her demands, then she gets even worse with the others and I'm terrified that if they get to the point where they've had enough and leave, that I'll be left there on my own with her. And I can't be 'that bastard that leaves his dying wife'. Plus, she plays up the fact that she's dying so often that we are all made to feel like we are obligated somehow to be kind to her, regardless of how she treats us in turn."

He finally met Petra's gaze and they reached out hands across the table to each other. "It's just an impossibly hard situation."

"Oh honey, I'm so sorry. Is there anything I can do?"

"Well, meeting up with you has been a breath of fresh air actually. I'm so grateful to have had this chance to catch up and talk with you. I've missed you a lot over the years... not that I've specifically thought about you for ages, but now... well I just realised how much you mean to me. Thank you for being here today. And for letting me talk so openly about my situation."

He signalled the waiter for the bill, settled it with a generous tip and they walked to her car.

"You know I really do mean it when I say I'm grateful to you for listening and understanding my situation. I'd forgotten how special you are to me." James hugged Petra and held her tight for just a little longer than might be necessary, but he felt like a man drowning who had suddenly found a life jacket floating past him. She finally broke the embrace and stepped back.

"James, honey, if you need to talk anytime, I'm only as far away as the other end of the phone ok. Do you do much on Facebook? "

"A bit – not much though. Can we connect there?"

"Yes, just add me as a friend, and we'll talk there ok? Might be easier than by phone if there are people in your house likely to listen in. But seriously, whatever happens, let's not let years go by before we catch up again ok? I've missed you." She leaned over and kissed him on the cheek before unlocking her car. James resisted the urge to hug her again, stopping only by putting his hands in his pockets. God, she'd felt so good.

All the way home, he thought about her, how she'd smelled when he'd held her, the way she'd gently held his hand in reassurance, her beautiful brown eyes that reminded him of shimmering maple syrup poured over pancakes, her long dark hair.... God he'd missed her these last few years.

Arriving home he found Alice in one of her usual moods of mostly feigned helplessness. Since the runaway incident, she'd been more demanding than ever. She stubbornly resisted any knowledge of having falling down the stairs in the middle of the night. Her attitude was that her medication must have made her sleepwalk one day, then the next she'd insist they were making it all up. "Don't you know I am *dying*. How can you even talk about such absurd ideas?" she would say in her plaintive and most helpless voice. Laying back on her pillows, she'd sigh, close her eyes, and then a few moments later flutter them open and demand to be carried downstairs to sit for a while, before fifteen minutes later changing her mind.

Meals were an increasingly challenging time. Some days she'd throw the food back at whomever brought up her tray. Other times she'd take two bites and then demand something else.

James was at his wits end as to how to deal with her. It had been delightful talking to Petra, but now, the enormity of his situation sat once again like a sack of bricks around his shoulders. After dinner that evening he logged onto his laptop and accepted a Facebook friend request from Petra.

J: Hi…

P: Hi yourself ☺

J: It was wonderful seeing you again today. I feel so uplifted by our conversation.

P: Yes I enjoyed it too. Very much. I'm so sorry for what's going on at home. No one deserves that. Is there nothing you can do?

J: Like what?

P: Well what about just calling her bluff and putting her into care?

J: Nice idea, but I think she's actually too smart for that, and not really mad enough to allow me to get away with it.

P: What do you mean?

J: Well let's just say I did that, and she managed to convince the medical staff that she was quite well enough to go home, and that her bastard of a husband was just trying to get rid of her. She could easily use a phone to call in a lawyer and do several things to damage me.

P: Really? Like what?

J: For a start, she could call many of our friends and her family and paint me out to be a total bastard. Now I may not like what I'm living with, but I really don't see why I should open myself up to that kind of drama. Secondly, she could change her will in such a way that when she does die, it would be incredibly difficult to untangle our financial matters inside a year and still leave me with a helluva lot less financial security. Now – that might sound somewhat mercenary, but imagine if she decided to leave her share of our joint estate to the cat's protection league for example. That would mean my having to sell our home, and have my business valued, and deal with Deanna's contesting the will most likely for her share, and then once that was all unravelled, I'd have not only a huge legal chunk taken out of my own dwindling share of 'our' estate after a year or so of legal wrangling, and why would I want to risk that after having gone through so much already?

P: I hadn't thought of that. Interesting!

J: And finally, after nearly three years of this, the end could in fact be only a few months away now.   I think after all this time I might be better to just ride it out.   I think the others might hopefully feel that way – but I was thinking after I left you today, that at least IF they decided they'd had enough, I could just increase the nurse's time here and hope for the best.

P: What did you mean by saying it might not be much longer now anyway?

J: Well a few months ago she did something a bit nutty – tried to run away in the middle of the night. So we had her tested for mental agility and found that there are some signs of dementia settling in. Also, her medication has changed and the cancer is a little more aggressive as a result.   But she can't go back on the other medication because she's allergic to it – which might explain why the onset of the dementia has happened so suddenly..   However it could also be argued that she just has selective memory loss when it suits her. Anyway –the upshot is, that now it might only be another three – six months until the end.

P: But haven't you been down that track before?

J: Yes but this time I think it might be different for a number of reasons.

P: Ok.   Well I think I might call it a night – it's been a long day.

J: Ok. Well thanks again for today. I, it really meant a lot to me to be able to catch up with you. Goodnight beautiful Petra. Xx

Petra looked at the sign off from James and hesitated. *'Beautiful Petra? XX'?* What was that about?

She finally posted: Goodnight – sleep well ok. ☺

That night James tossed and turned, trying desperately to get to sleep. But it eluded him and he lay awake thinking about the day before. Mostly he thought about Petra and how it had felt to hold her in that hug. Her hair against his face, how it had smelled so fresh and felt so silky. How her body had yielded into the hug, with her warm arms hugging him back. He felt his cock twitch in anticipation of going further down that path of remembrance and slid his hand down under the sheets to grab it.

Even that didn't help him to get to sleep. A little while later he was still staring at the ceiling. Finally he turned on the light and grabbed his laptop. Facebook winked into life and the screen stared back at him as he started to type.

Petra, I have to clarify a few things, as I said today, Alice and I fell out of love about ten years ago, We stayed together in a sexless, courteous marriage because... I'm not really sure why. I moved into the spare room eight years ago, and to be honest the lack of sex was not really so important at the time. I got on with my workaholic ways, Alice with her shopping and collecting. And we co-existed in our separate lives until the cancer came along. For a while I found a new love for her – more like as a sister – and with that at the time a true desire to be there for her through the cancer thing till the bitter end. Back then we thought it was only a few months. In the meantime I've learned a lot about myself. You of course must know I've always really liked you. I have always and still do find you to be an incredibly attractive woman, with drive and intellect, kindness and a compassion that is so heart-warming. But I have never been sure where you stood as far as your view of me. After talking with you today though (yesterday now sorry) I realised this might be the time when you might be free and I might be on the verge of being so too...and where we can perhaps be more than just friends. Maybe now is the moment. If this is the case, then is a gentle approach best, or do we just go for it? Oops – I'd better find out if you just want to remain as friends or see where this could lead to? So there it is, my heart is open and my truth is told. No games. Your move. Love James

James eased back onto his pillow, barely having realised how tense he had been while typing the long note. He read it back slowly. Should he send it? Would she respond? Did she really know how he felt? But what if he didn't and she went off and found someone else to … he couldn't bear to put the thought into words. Well, if that was the case, it would still be better to have her know how he felt about her. Not that he was quite sure himself.

He took a deep breath and pushed send. "Oh God – what if she…" what if she what? He asked himself for the third or fourth time. "What if she responded positively? Or negatively? Was he risking a special friendship?" No he decided. Either way, he would not be comfortable seeing Petra again without her knowing how he felt about her. That would be too difficult. And if she wanted to be only good friends, then he was sure she'd be quite understanding of his feelings for her and they were close enough that it would not matter too much really. Maybe they'd still be closer?

With that thought playing through his mind he finally drifted off to sleep.

CHAPTER 12

Petra smoothed back her hair, smudged her lips together, grabbed her bag off the seat, made her way to the café opposite the marina, and found a seat in the corner. Tapping her foot restlessly, she debated changing chairs to face away from the door, asked the waiter for water and a cup of Earl Grey tea then looked up to see James walking towards her with a smile.

Should she stand up and hug him, or sit and wait for him to take a seat? The waiter was standing between them, so that made it easy to decide to stay seated. She adjusted the collar on her blue shirt, and shook out her hair a little, never breaking eye contact.

"Hi."

"Hi yourself."

They had greeted each other this way for years she realised. So much history tied up in two letters.

James sat down and studied her carefully, seeking any sign of... what? Discomfort, anxiety, happiness at seeing him?

What did he want from this meeting? Certainty for one thing. Some surety that she might feel the same way about him? Was there a chance of that or would they forever be destined to just be great friends. He had reasoned with himself that if that was the case, he'd never allow such distance and time to separate them again. And certainly not any other woman in his future either.

Forcing all those thoughts into the far reaches of his mind for the moment, he smiled. "So, have you been waiting long?"

"All my life actually." Her look was intense, and she licked then rolled her lips in that way that she did, that made him suddenly ache to lean over and kiss her.

"Oh, really?" Stuck for words – not like him at all really. But it was not every day the woman you'd spent years thinking about, actually spoke directly to his heart in such a way that he felt he might burst forth with all the words he'd ever thought about saying to her. In a heartbeat he imagined himself doing exactly that and exploding in the room amid a flash bomb of letters falling like snow on everyone in the room. The image was enough to make him grin at the comedic idea. He had glanced down for a moment but raised his eyes to look back into Petra's deep brown depths.

Reaching into his pocket he drew out a twenty dollar bill, tossed it on the table to cover their drinks order and stood up. "I think we should get out of here and walk on the beach don't you?"

Petra nodded, standing in agreement and within moments they were walking barefoot along the beach, each swaying their shoes in one hand, and holding on to each other's hand. James had once read somewhere that a deep and meaningful conversation was always much easier had when two people were not facing each other, but standing, sitting, walking, or driving side by side. This was certainly the case today, and the words from both poured forth easily as they explored more of their typed conversations of the past three weeks.

While Petra had been away in New South Wales on business, they had explored a huge amount of general knowledge about each other's past ten years. She had grown to understand the reality of his loveless marriage leading up to his decision to leave Alice, only days before she was diagnosed with terminal cancer. He had learned more about her own failed relationships and dreams of a better future leading to her moving to the Gold Coast.

Their conversations, although typed as instant messages and not spoken, were intensely personal, and covered a lot of areas of each of their lives. From cooking and money, to sex and masturbation, no stone was left unturned. And now, following on from a decision that they wanted to see if there was any potential at all for a relationship, they were walking on the beach, ignoring the gulls and children, feeling only the wind in their hair, and the sun on their bodies.

"Petra, I have to say this. I know that I'm not in a position to offer you anything at all, I'm married and locked into a situation that I cannot see my way out of within the next few months. But – while I'm standing here, looking at you and hoping that you really do feel the way I do about a possible future for us together, please know that I will do everything in my power to make that happen. And when that does happen, I will love you and commit to you and to US for forever."

Petra reached up and pulled him to her, kissing him gently on his lips. He hesitated for the barest moment, aware that they were publicly visible, then not caring at all as his every wish came true. She was soft, and sweet, and as her lips moved gently in their search of his, and he tasted the salt on her and breathed in the scent of her, he knew he'd found home.

Breaking apart after a few moments, he hugged her to him, and fought back tears as he realised that his life had just changed for the better.

"James, what will happen if Alice gets better again?"

"If Alice gets better again I'll leave. I have to. I cannot stay like this for much longer. But as I said last week, I have hopes that we may finally be looking at the end this time. Since her change in medication, she has become a little frailer and has agreed finally to go into hospital for some tests to determine exactly where her cancer is at right now. There are options for surgery, alternative medicines and therapies, but in the past she'd not wanted these saying that they were too invasive. And yet she keeps lingering in this place of... of... God I have no idea how to describe it."

He led her to large rock for them to both sit on and once they were comfortable he continued, after briefly kissing her again. "She sits in her bed, ordering everyone about, refuses to do anything for herself, including options to help extend her life. I call it the Cleopatra existence. If there were slaves to wave fans over her and peel grapes she'd probably want that too. She shops on the home shopping network for things that she often doesn't even unwrap – and so Deanna eventually returns them or sometimes keeps them for herself or Maddie. Thank God she hasn't discovered online gambling or we'd really be in the shit. But she's *mean*, to everyone except her cat. She's certainly not the woman I married once, and while there have been shades of this selfishness for many years now, the worse her health gets, the worse she becomes."

He heaved a big sigh. "Petra, I can't go on like this. I simply can't. And I'm ready to move forward in my own life and want to be with you... if you'll have me?"

Petra shifted and leaned forward so she could take both his hands in hers before replying. Looking deep into his eyes, she simply said: "Yes James, I'm ready too".

PART
TWO

A Woman Scorned

Winter 2010

CHAPTER 13

Alice shifted uncomfortably in her bed. The pillows needed fluffing up better or something. "Deanna. Deanna… come and sort out my pillows will you?"

Deanna put down her crossword puzzle and adjusted the offending pillows, smoothed the blankets, and glared at her mother. She was so fed up she could barely stand it a minute longer. 'Do this, do that.' It was constant, and Alice was so ungrateful it was all she could to not to slap her.

"I want to go downstairs. Where's James? He'll have to carry me!"

"Why do you even bother? You'll only want to come back up in twenty minutes? Just stay there."

"Where's James? James? James come in here now!"

"You can call out all you like but he won't come." Deanna sat back down and picked up her crossword, doing her best to ignore Alice's calling out to a James who was not even home.

A few minutes later Brett walked in. "What's the matter Alice?"

"I want James. I want to go downstairs and sit in the lounge."

Brett looked at Deanna, who looked back and then rolled her eyes in annoyance. "I can take you downstairs."

"I want James. Where is he anyway? He's supposed to be here in the afternoons."

"James is out, he's busy, and will be home for dinner. You can see him then. Now do you want to go downstairs or not?"

"Yes," she snapped.

Brett took the blankets off and bent down to lift her. 'Jeez she can't be much more than forty kilos', he thought. He was quite surprised at her feather weight, having known her when she was a healthy size 12. They'd made it to the top of the stairs when Alice whimpered, causing him to stop before starting their descent. "Are you ok?" She sniffed. "Alice?"

"No," was all she said.

"'No' what Alice? No you are not ok, or what?" For all that she was light as a feather, she was not easy to hold, and he didn't like the way she smelled either. Carrying her downstairs was something he usually avoided, but this time he'd wanted to deflect her mind from dwelling on James's absence. He said a quick silent prayer hoping his friend was having a lovely time with the beautiful Petra.

"No I don't want to go downstairs."

"Are you sure?"

"Yes."

He rolled his own eyes at Deanna as he took her back to her bed. Bloody woman – God she was impossible to please as always but Brett was sure it was even worse lately. Since returning from the hospital a week ago where she'd gone for tests to determine her current state of health and wellbeing, she was particularly mean when she got the chance.

"Get out you both – I want to sleep for a while. I hate being watched by you bloody vultures while I'm sleeping. Go on – out you go."

Deanna didn't need telling twice, and was out the door ahead of Brett. They met up in the kitchen and fell about laughing. "See I told you. She's worse than ever!" Brett grinned and started the kettle to boil for a cup of tea.

"I sure hope James is having a good time - he'll sure as eggs have to deal with the Spanish inquisition when he gets back." Deanna grabbed two cups and put them on the bench.

"Yes, me too. God what a crazy stupid situation. Still I'm glad he's taking a big more control of his own life and getting out a bit more. Mum has been such a bitch I'm surprised he hadn't thrown her bloody pillows over her head yet." She laughed for a moment. "That would be a tough investigation wouldn't it. Who had the most motive and opportunity to do the old girl in?"

Brett heard the words spoken in jest but felt a cold shiver run up his spine. "Yes, who indeed?" there was a cautionary part of him that wanted to have Alice in hospital as soon as possible so that should anything go wrong at all, or if any of the three of them give into temptation to do just that, they would not find themselves caught up in such an investigation. "Remember how bad it was when the cops thought one of us might have pushed her down the stairs last year? It would be a hundred times worse if anything happened to Alice here."

"What do you mean?"

"Well if she's in hospital, and anything goes wrong it would be a medical issue, not something coming back to bite any of us in the arse." The clock in the hallway chimed, shaking him from the awful thoughts that had suddenly started running through his mind.

"Oh, I see what you mean…" Deanna poured the tea and they both sat at the table, sipping quietly for a few minutes.

"Do you think she'll die soon?" Deanna broke the silence.

"I don't really know love, but I sure do hope so, for all our sakes! I mean how can she call this a life? It's a total waste, for all of us."

"I admire people who get out and make the most of every minute they are still here when they are given a death sentence – don't you? I mean, Mum just lingers. And she's spiteful. I really don't know how James has coped for so long."

"Well he has us to get him through it – that's the reality. I think if he wasn't such a good guy, and didn't have us to share this with he'd have shot her *and* himself years ago."

Brett stood up and put his cup in the dishwasher, leaving Deanna to her thoughts. Thoughts that mostly were about Alice's medication.

CHAPTER 14

The next day, James woke up from a deep sleep to find his phone ringing insistently. It was only 5am.

"Brett, what's up? It's like, still dark."

"Buddy I need to tell you about the conversation that happened yesterday between me and Deanna. I didn't get a chance to last night. But I think it's important. So – as soon as the nurse arrives, let's get out of here and go for coffee ok?"

"Sure, no problem – see you soon." James hung up, and fell back on his pillow wondering what that had been all about. He hoped like hell Deanna wasn't planning to move out. They'd all be lost without her.

The next two hours dragged by, made marginally shorter only by some texting between him and Petra. He could barely believe his luck that he had found the love of his life and that she felt the same. They were both so similar, and their years of close friendship certainly helped in terms of getting to know each other even better. In fact, she was extraordinary, he decided. And he felt so incredibly calm with her.

Ninety minutes later Brett and James were nursing coffees at a local café overlooking the beach, watching some early morning surfers enjoy the early morning waves. Some were older men like themselves who met each morning for a surf before heading into the city to work, but most were young students making the most of the end of summer holidays - they would be out on the ocean for as long as their hunger pains and thirst allowed them to. Brett looked at them with envy wondering why after so many years living here he'd still not learned to surf – something he'd talked about doing for years.

Turning his attention to his friend, he cleared his throat for dramatic effect, before starting to speak. "Buddy, I'm not sure that we're not all in a very difficult position with Alice living at home in the state she's in." He paused to take a sip of his coffee, while James looked at him with eyebrows raised slightly. He was used to Brett's flair for drama, and decided to just wait and see where this was going.

"Yesterday Alice was making a fuss about things as usual, and Deanna was clearly at her breaking point, over it all, but she made some comments later downstairs about if anything was to happen to Alice, we'd all be investigated. Well that got me thinking that maybe she's right. What if any of us got fed up and clocked her one – and God knows I've thought about it once or twice." He laughed as though to make light of the comment, but James knew there was an undercurrent of truth to the idea. "Well there would be a helluva lot of explaining to do wouldn't there?"

"Exactly what are you trying to say Brett?"

"Well, if anything happened to Alice now, there are three or four of us who would be investigated thoroughly and maybe that would be a much bigger nightmare than the one we're already living through. Can we get her out of the house and put her into care?"

"God I wish it was that easy." James drained his cup and signaled to the waiter to come over.

"But why is it not?"

76

James ordered another coffee with the hovering waiter and turned back to Brett. "Because, she's not quite sick enough yet to be in full time care, and when she is lucid and at her worst, she's still able to make it sound as though we, or at least I, am trying to take advantage of her. If she was to keep improving, then her ending up in a care facility might just backfire on me enormously. Plus, if she was to find out about Petra, then there'd be absolute hell to pay. But... having said that, maybe we should be doing something to speed things along a little. I mean, I'm completely over this torture."

"Me too Buddy – so over it. And I'm sure Deanna has thought about taking things further to – Alice is so incredibly hard work and Dee just wants done with it all."

"So what are you suggesting?"

"Well I don't know, but I am sure we have to do something. We simply can't keep doing this for another year or two."

Their eggs and bacon arrived, followed quickly by more coffee, they turned their attention to eating, but each was thinking hard about the possibilities of bringing their circumstances to a new outcome sooner rather than later.

CHAPTER 15

Petra was sure someone was following her. How was that possible? And who could have any reason to do so? But the eerie feeling of being watched was becoming unnerving. It was not all the time, but certainly often enough that she was becoming unnaturally jumpy.

She'd always felt quite safe living in Surfers Paradise, and had in fact moved there for that small city feeling she'd enjoyed during holidays over the years. The decision to actually relocate her life there was made quite quickly, but once made, everything had fallen into place so well it was as though the universe was in full support of the move and rolling out the red carpet for her.

Work was easy - as a freelance designer she could take her clients and work potential anywhere. Her living arrangements were also easy, as she had no dependents to care about any more with her children all grown up and traveling the world. Reconnecting with James as a friend first and now as lovers, was an added bonus. Petra had always enjoyed excellent friendships with both men and women, and had never considered James to be anything more than a good friend, but found that their connection was in fact extraordinary on all levels now, and she was wondering how she'd missed the signs of their potential to be more than just great mates all these years.

The biggest concern now was how to advance their relationship while his wife was dying, albeit taking a very long time to do so. How was that going to work out for them? It was clear to both that even if Alice was to pass away tomorrow, too many people would assume they had been happily married for years and that therefore James would be a concerned and grieving husband for at least a decent amount of time after her passing. The reality was that in most cases, spouses did grieve for their significant other for a long time, even when the relationship was not always a great one. The challenge for James and Petra though was the fact that Alice kept hovering at about the 70% point of dying, and had been doing so for years. Who knew how long it could continue this way? And where did that leave Petra?

She acknowledged that James was not able to leave his wife – that would be grossly unfair and would no doubt cost him a lot of goodwill among friends and family, not to mention his business might also suffer. But at the same time, did she Petra want to have nothing more than an affair with him for the foreseeable medium term?

Petra turned the light on in the kitchen and grabbed a glass out of the cupboard. The drapes were all drawn, the doors were locked, and there was no one around, but the feeling of being watched remained. She returned to her room, and rechecked the windows and doors again on the way to bed, then climbed under the covers and grabbed her mobile to check the battery. Wishing she could call James for some reassurance, but opting to send a text instead, she finally decided to leave the bathroom light on before trying to get some sleep.

CHAPTER 16

James sat on the bed beside Alice, and held her hand. This was going to be a difficult conversation, but it had to be had. "Darling, I hope you've enjoyed your lunch. Are you warm enough?"

Alice was in a good mood, and eyed him like a small child who thinks the adult has candy in their pocket. "I'm fine thank you. And yes lunch was lovely – thank you for making it specially, you know how much I adore your soups. Now – tell me about your day, how's everything in your business?"

"Well business is quite good at the moment actually. It's been great having the extra time to put into it lately, and that makes a difference. Plus I'm enjoying being out of the house a bit more." He looked at her carefully as he let those words sink in, expecting some kind of reaction, but unsure how his comments would go down exactly. She continued to look at him as though she may not have heard or understood him, so he continued. "I'm actually wanting to find a way for us to make it easier for us all to cope with these changes my darling. I want to talk about improving the level of care you are getting now." He finally saw the dark shadow pass her eyes as she grasped the direction of the conversation. Plunging on he decided to rip the band aid off, - there was going to be hell to pay however he put it so decided to just get on with it.

"Alice, darling, I want us to talk about putting you into care." As the words came sweetly out of his mouth, he mentally backed two feet away from the bed, but remained holding her hand calmly and looking at her gently.

"You bastard. You utter fucking bastard! How dare you? What the hell do you think you are doing? I won't go. I simply won't and you can't make me. I'll fight you all the way to my deathbed on this, you bastard!!!" Her volume was rising and there was a screech in her voice as her tirade gathered momentum. "Is Deanna in on this? Brett? I'm not sick enough to be cared for. There's no way I will do this. NO way. I just won't. Deanna, Deanna, get in here you little bitch. DEANNA!"

"Deanna is out and so is Brett, there's only me here this evening Alice." James was doing his best to remain calm and keep his voice level, but inside he was panicking about her reaction. He'd expected it to be dramatic, but suddenly wished he'd arranged for the others to be there and jointly explain this to her. "Darling I feel that…"

"Don't you call me that! I'm not your 'darling' James. I'm nothing to you, and you don't even care that I'm dying. You just want to throw me into a nursing home. Have you seen those places? I wouldn't put a dog there. How can you possibly think I'll let you put me into a nursing home? I'm not even *that* sick yet."

"Actually, you are unable to get out of bed without help, you can't care for yourself, and we, all of us, are at our wits end trying to care for you all the time. Deanna is still a young woman and needs to be living her own life, not chained here to this house and your demands, and…"

"She's a spoiled little bitch who doesn't even care that her own mother is dying. She can get stuffed. I don't need her. We don't need her. We can cope James, you and I, and Brett…"

"Brett is ready to move out at a moment's notice!"

"But he's my friend. He told me he'll be here until I go. I don't believe you. You bastard. You think you can stoop to doing this to me and putting doubt into my friendships too? I'll not let you James."

"ALICE, will you listen to me? We are ALL of us, ALL of us completely and utterly at the end of our tethers over your demands and your bad attitude." James stood up and put his hands on his hips as he yelled at her. Not caring anymore, he threw caution to the wind and delivered his final statement on the matter. "An assessment team will be here in the morning. Good night!"

As he left the room, he had to stop himself from slamming the door behind him, but was shaking uncontrollably by the time he got to the kitchen and opened the fridge door seeking the white wine left over from the previous evening. Not bothering to get a glass, he simply slumped in a chair and upended the bottle to drain the remaining half a glass. Just then Brett and Deanna walked in. Seeing his face, they both stopped talking and sat down.

"Was it bad buddy?" Brett didn't know what else to say. He'd known all day that James was going to tell Alice about the assessment team from the home coming the next day, but it was all news to Deanna. Brett quickly filled her in after James just nodded his reply.

Deanna got up and put the kettle on, then changed her mind and reached into the cupboard for the Jack Daniels and poured them all a glass full. "So, were you going to talk with me about this at some time?"

"Yes Dee, but it all came together today with Rest Haven and so I didn't really get a chance to. But I think it's for the best don't you? I mean none of us can keep this up. It's just too hard."

"Well yes, but it might be that she's really dying this time. I mean, what if she is? What if we're down to only a few weeks left?" Deanna was confused by the idea and as much as she was learning to despise her mother, she was torn over what was the right thing to do by her.

"But we don't know that do we. She refuses to even go back into hospital and have any updated tests. She could be in remission for all we know, or she could just as easily drop dead overnight. And not knowing is driving all of us into the ground."

"Dee, I know I can't keep doing this any longer – I'm done. I'm only staying out of loyalty to you both," said Brett. If I have to face another six months of this I'll go mad, and I've got it a lot easier than you two do."

"Face facts Deanna, this is the end. And Alice has to realise that too."

"Do you think she'll make it totally horrible now?" Deanna was clearly not convinced this was the best option but wasn't opposed to the idea either.

"Oh yes, I think we're about to see a whole new side to Alice now." James drained his glass and said goodnight leaving the others to talk quietly about this new development.

CHAPTER 17

"James, James, Jeezus buddy – wake up, what did you lock your door for?   James, for God's sake, would you..." James opened the door, pulling his dressing gown on sleepily. "What's the matter, it's still...what time is it?"

Ignoring him, Brett pushed past into James's bedroom and sat on the bed, then stood again, letting out a deep moan.   "Jeezus James, what the hell were you *thinking*?"

"What the hell are you talking about? What's going on?"

"Alice, it's Alice, she's... what do you mean what's going on?"

James by now was wearing an expression common to people woken in the morning by hysterical people who don't actually say what they are upset about. "Brett, for God's sake, would you sit down, shut up and tell me what the hell you are going on about! What about Alice?"

Glancing at the clock he could see it was a little after 5.30 am, maybe a little early for Brett who normally was the first awake in the house most days. However usually he'd be sitting outside with a cup of coffee and a cigarette to start the day with at this hour.   The home nurse was due at 6.30 to get Alice started for the day with a shower, change of bed wear and then breakfast.

Brett was sitting, but shaking his head and slightly shaking. As jittery as a rat in a restaurant.

Rolling his eyes, James quickly decided to leave Brett there and go and see what was wrong with Alice. Not having returned to her room after her hysterical outburst the night before, he was unsure what to expect, but wondered as he climbed the stairs if she'd hurled herself out of bed and wrecked her room or something. Maybe she'd fallen and no one had heard her? He usually slept with his door open in case of such a thing, but last night he had just wanted to close himself away from the whole world, locking it out had been an unconscious decision.

Entering her room, he noted the light was on beside her bed, he froze when he saw her still form, with a pillow over her face. "Oh fuck!" he said quietly. Moving quickly, he crossed the room and took the pillow away, expecting to see her eyes wide open and a deathly stare, but found instead she looked like she was asleep. He wanted to shake her but decided instead to check for her pulse. None there. Damn. But she was warm. Pulling the covers back, he put his hand on her heart, feeling again for any sign of life. *'Maybe...'* thoughts of Alan Alda in MASH flashed through his mind as he grabbed a mirror from her dressing table and holding it to her mouth, he called out to Brett and Deanna. Alice was breathing – but it was shallow, and she was definitely not waking.

"Brett, call an ambulance, dammit. Deanna? Are you there? For fuck's sake you guys, call a bloody ambulance!" He wasn't sure if she needed mouth to mouth, she was after all breathing, but should he do CPR? No, that was silly – her heart was clearly still beating. How the HELL did this happen? He looked at the face of his wife, and then at the pillow, and suddenly realised what this meant.

"Oh My GOD!!! Fuck! You bastards, which one of you bastards did this? For chrissakes…" He looked once more at Alice, who was still showing no obvious sign of life, and raced back to his room to find Brett still sitting on his bed, smoking a cigarette.

"Did you do it? Put that fucking cigarette out – get it OUT of my room. Jesus Brett, did you do it?"

Brett turned away from the window where he'd thrown the cigarette, eyes wide open. "NO, of course I didn't do it. I thought YOU did it."

They both looked at each other, then in unison said, "Deanna."

Racing through to the other end of the house, they didn't even hesitate at Deanna's door but barged straight in to find her fast asleep, earbuds still in playing loud music that sounded like a bee buzzing in her room. Their bursting in caused her to wake up instantly, and rise to a sitting position. There was enough early morning light coming through the window so they could easily see the shocked and very pissed off expression on her face.

"Deanna, did you see Alice last night?" questioned James.

"What the hell are you guys doing in my room!!?" Deanna went from zero to maximum yell by the third word.

"When was the last time you saw Alice?" James repeated the question. Not quite matching her tone or volume, but causing her to stop yelling and turn the light on beside her bed, she reached for a robe and swung her legs out of bed in one smooth movement.

"Last night – I checked her before I came to bed. Why what's wrong with her now?"

"Are you sure?"

"Of course I'm bloody sure. Would one of you fuck wits tell me what the hell is going on?"

"Jesus!" Brett rolled his eyes and wondered what the hell to actually say. James saved him from having to do more than think about it.

"She's lying up there with a fucking pillow over her face, barely alive. One of us," he looked quickly at the others with open hostility written all over his face, "has clearly decided to take matters into their own hands and speed up the process. But – she's still alive and the pillow was still there this morning. So would one of you or both of you kindly tell me what the hell prompted you to do it?"

"You mean she's still alive?" Brett's voice squeaked in horror as he digested this information.

"She's breathing – but only just. Fuck – we'd better call an ambulance." James stormed from the room to find the phone and make the call, leaving Brett and Deanna eyeing each other suspiciously.

"What did you do that for if you weren't going to do the job properly?" Deanna glared at Brett and went upstairs to her mother's room. Brett followed quickly. "What did *I* do? I didn't do anything. What is it with you two that you think I've done this? Just because I found her. I thought *you* must have done it."

"Me, why the hell would I do that? And," she turned on the stairs and glared at him, pointing a straight finger as his face. "If it was me, I'd have certainly not done a half-arsed job of it, you can be bloody sure of that!"

They entered the bedroom and found Alice still lying as James had left her a few moments earlier, looking for all the world as though she was *dead* asleep. "Mum, can you hear me, Mum, are you awake? Mum, it's me Deanna, wake up now Mum." Holding her hand and then deciding to shake her a little instead, Alice was completely unresponsive.

"Fuck!" Brett was unsure what to do, but thought he should at least say something and 'Fuck' was the only word that seemed to want to come out of his mouth.

James walked in, phone in hand, obviously talking to the dispatcher. "No, she's completely unresponsive.... Deanna, can you please try and take a pulse... Yes, we found her like this this morning. No, she wasn't up in the night. No we don't have a night nurse arrangement. Yes she was fine at about ... Dee what time did you check on her?"

"About 10.20 pm"

"She was checked on at 10.20 by her daughter and was fine then." He raised his eyebrows in question as he said that and Deanna nodded.

"Thank you, yes someone will wait on the foot path – yes, yes, thank you." James finished the call. "Right – ambulance will be here in about two minutes and one of us has to go wait for it, now – both of you – outside!" He quickly glanced at Alice and then ushered them out to the hallway quickly.

"Are you both trying to say that neither of you deliberately tried to end Alice's life last night? Because if so, we better all get our bloody stories straight hadn't we?" Brett and Deanna nodded quickly and silently. "Let's agree we don't make any mention of the pillow ok?" More nodding. "Brett, why did you come in so early to check on her then?"

"I saw the light was on and thought she must be awake so thought I'd better ask if she wanted a cup of tea – and found her. I thought you must have... Well... I just panicked and came to you."

"OK. Just go wait for the ambulance ok? I'd better get dressed and ride along with her, unless you want to Dee?"

Deanna shook her head and muttered that she was going to go back to bed once the day nurse had been let go.

Hell Hath No Fury

CHAPTER 18

Deanna was scared and it was not a feeling she was used to. The police had turned up again and asked a mountain of questions, and she had no answers at all for any of them. The mystery of who had obviously tried to kill her mother was weighing heavily on her mind. Who did it? Her mind was as busy as any reader of an Agatha Christie novel, but still nothing made sense.

What was worse, not knowing if the police actually suspected anything or if they were maybe just fishing for something unknown? All she really knew in that regard was that they had arrived and asked if she was aware of anything untoward in regards to her mother having to be rushed into hospital that morning. In fact they were very unspecific by saying they were just making routine enquiries.

She'd laughed for a moment when 'Inspector Plod' had pulled out his notebook and said those words, The ones she'd remembered from every bad cop film she'd ever watched where that phrase was used. Often in those shows, this was followed up within thirty minutes by the bad guy swearing at the cops as he was lowered into a waiting squad car. Here she was now dealing with her own version of a Buster Keaton silent movie.

After they left she was once again alone with her thoughts. 'Could James really have become so fed up that he was ready to end it all?' What a risk! No, she was pretty sure that he not only didn't have the balls for such a move, but would have been very aware of the consequences of such a move. In fact, the very suspicion of it would have been enough to stop him from acting on such an impulse she thought.

So that left Brett.

Brett was many things, but certainly not a killer, regardless of how far pushed. Besides, he was totally freaked out about it all. In the few hours since the drama unfolded, she had seen him break down at least twice and sob like a baby.

The Machiavellian side of her kicked in for a moment and considered another angle. Was it possible that Brett appeared so upset because he was covering up his actions by *pretending* to be so shocked? Throwing that around in her mind for a moment or two brought her right back to where she had started from. Which of the two men she shared a home with, could possibly have felt such murderous rage required to actually try and kill her mother?

Well, to be honest, at this stage she deserved everything she got! The mean streak in Deanna resurfaced and she thought back yet again over all the horrible ways that Alice had made their collective lives totally miserable lately.

As she'd told 'Inspector Plod' when she did the final check on her mother last night Alice had been sitting up with her light on, reading something – no she didn't know what exactly – and said a grumpy goodnight when Deanna asked if she needed anything before she went to bed.

That was the last time she'd seen her and *no*, there were no other calls during the night, and *no*, Alice did not seem in any way different than at the end of any other miserable day in her life.

The phone ringing jolted her out of the mental gymnastics she was now doing in her head.

"Hello Brett, what's happening?"

"Hi." Such a forlorn sounding greeting. Was that a cover up or a genuine sound? 'Stop it!' Deanna quickly admonished herself for where her thoughts had instantly taken her.

"Hi. Is everything ok?"

She could hear Brett draw a deep breath. 'Oh no, please stop bloody crying!' she thought. "She's ok, but in a coma. And they aren't sure if she'll pull out of it or not." He sniffed. She rolled her eyes. "Oh! Well … that's big. Um, do we need to all be there?" She asked while wracking her mind quickly to see if the 'right' thing to do would pop quickly into her mind, but found it was vacant.

"No, they say she's resting comfortably, but there's no sign of her coming round just at the moment and they don't know if this will change quickly or not. They are saying that as she's pulled through the first few hours or so it's a good sign, and her health was pretty good in some ways before this. She wasn't really at death's door this week. So I guess it's a wait and see situation."

"Ok." Deanna wasn't sure what else to say.

Brett continued, but dropped his voice conspiratorially. "Hey, have you been thinking about what happened?"

Deanna suppressed a laugh. "Um, Brett, the police were just here, I've been thinking very hard about it all. How about you?" She wondered yet again if he might know a lot more than he pretended about the whole situation. She was stopped from continuing by what sounded like James interrupting Brett on the other end of the phone. Then he was speaking to her.

"Hey Dee, I think it would be great if you could come to the hospital and relieve Brett from being here, and then later if he can relieve me so I can come home and take a shower. Is that ok?" He sounded very business-like and she thought of his wonderful calm in the face of any emergency and for a moment the thought of him in a ship captain's uniform barking directions from the bridge.

"Yeah sure – I can be there in about forty-five minutes. Hey the police were here just before."

"They were?"

"Yeah, asking about how Mum was last night, and a few 'routine questions'. I don't know anything, and didn't really know how to answer them but they didn't stay long. I... well, I..." James cut in.

"Yes Dee I know, it's a bit of an odd situation isn't it?"

He'd cut her off before she could ask anything of him and she filed that away in her mind for later thought.

An hour later, the three of them were standing in the Relatives' Room, eyeing each other somewhat warily. One of them had tried to kill Alice, but which one? Each was suspicious of the other two, and yet no one spoke.

James finally broke the silence. "Ok, there's a big fat white elephant in this room, so who wants to poke it first?"

The other two shifted uncomfortably in their chairs and looked away. "Oh, come on!" James was not prepared to let this go, and his white knuckled grip on the arms of his chair should have been a clear sign to the others that he was also feeling somewhat aggrieved at them both. He finally made eye contact with Deanna. "Deanna, I am pretty sure Brett didn't do this, and I know I didn't, so that leaves you! Sorry but that's the way it is."

Deanna instantly scowled and had she been standing, a foot stomp would have been an appropriate match for her face. "James, how the hell can you say that? I have been thinking that *you* have the most to gain out of this!"

"Oh no you don't! I can't believe you would think that!" James snorted and looked away, then back again and this time targeted Brett with a hard stare. "Brett, what do you think?"

At this, Brett yet again welled up with tears that quickly overflowed his eyes, raining down on his cheeks. He wiped his face and gulped. Trying hard not to sob, he took a long moment to pull himself together, then finally said to them both: "I refuse to believe any of us could do this...and not do it *properly*!"

At that they all laughed, and nervous tension evaporated immediately. Brett snorted in relief and the next thing they were all giggling like loons so hard that a nurse put her head round the door to see what was causing the hysteria. She quickly left, and they all looked at each other again and resumed their laughter, slowly collecting themselves and growing calm again.

"Oh my God, I think I needed that!" Brett wiped his face, and relaxed in his chair, almost slouching.

"Yes, I think I did too. Wow. I haven't laughed like that in years." Deanna smiled and the lack of tension seemed to take at least five years off her face.

"Ok, so let's talk this through ok? There's obviously something we all need to address. If none of us did attempt murder the other night, then we have to work out how Alice ended up here in a coma. I know that I didn't do it, and I'm kinda sorry for what I've been thinking and wondering about you both since yesterday." said James.

"Brett, James, I'm sorry too. I did wonder what on earth might have made one of you snap, and didn't really seriously think you did it. But I know I didn't and I couldn't think beyond the idea that one of you must have," confessed Deanna.

"Deanna, James, I have known you both for so long, and we've gone through a lot together already, so I can't imagine any of us doing this. Although I have to say, Alice has been getting increasingly difficult to live with, I still didn't think she was worth bumping off just yet." Brett smiled at them both.

He loved them both, and loved living with them. The thought that either of them had tried to kill Alice was the worst possible thing as far as he was concerned, as that would have meant a dramatic change to their lives in so many ways, and he hated change.

"So if none of us did this, and there was no one else in the house, then how did this happen?" Deanna let the question hang in the air for a long moment. None of them wanted to voice the possibilities that each was turning over hard in their minds. Could Alice really have done this to herself? If so, Why?

CHAPTER 19

Petra was the happiest she'd been in a very long time. In fact, she could not remember ever having felt this good. Her work was going well, her relationship with James was an unexpected bonus, and she was packing to go on a three day silent retreat in the mountains where she expected to find some inner peace and tranquility so that her next phase of goal setting and planning for the year ahead would be made easier.

This was something she tried to do every year so that at the end of each year she could mark off a few *'want to do's'* and *'must do's'* from her list of great living ideals. Some people called it a bucket list, for her, it was as much about *'things that matter'*, as it was about a wish list of things *'to do before I die'*. Always a planner, one thing she was also trying to do as she got older was to allow for semi-planned spontaneity, and this retreat opening was a last minute opportunity.

She left a message for James on his phone, and headed west, assuming it would only be a three hour drive to reach her destination. She had done several retreats before, all spiritually based, and for up to ten days, but this was her first experience of it being a fully silent retreat. Not good at being a silent being she was unsure her ability to get through a full three days without talking but was optimistic anyway.

As she drove, listening to her favourite music, she contemplated the situation with James and Alice. Obviously at some point in the reasonably near future Alice was likely to die. She had no particular feelings of warmth or even regret on Alice's behalf. From what she'd learned so far of the woman whose husband she was now completely in love with, Alice was better off gone from their lives. She trusted James when he said that if his wife returned to even a reasonable level of health 'this time round' he was now ready to leave her, but it still didn't seem fair on anyone should that be the outcome. After all, for having stuck by her for so long, his reputation as a good man and loving husband would be shot to bits if he walked out on a wife who was supposedly facing terminal cancer. That was the dilemma. Should he stay and risk this all lasting another year or two, or cut his losses and hope for the best? At least at this moment, the options were skewed further in the likelihood that she would not last a lot longer. But – as for the way she'd ended up in this state.... Wow. Her mind was still trying to process it all when she arrived at the Sun Maya Retreat two hours later.

Having checked in, and been instructed on the rules of the establishment, she attended the introductory meditation before dinner, then turned in early. To make it easier for everyone, each attendee was given their own room, which in itself was a different way to attend a retreat for Petra. In other retreats the women usually shared a room and it was a great opportunity to meet a new friend. However, she had to concede that a *silent* retreat would be incredibly difficult if networking at any level was encouraged.

The next day passed with a sunrise meditation, followed by breakfast, then yoga. The afternoon was spent in quiet reflection, before another meditation and dinner. Lights out was 8 pm, to ensure it was easier to be up at four-thirty for sunrise meditation the next day.

At first Petra knew with absolute certainty she was having a dream. As she watched like an outside observer, the scene unfolded before her and she kept telling herself that it was a dream even as the horse rode faster and faster towards her. She stood her ground and waited. The horse neared closer and she could see a rider wearing a cape and brandishing a long staff high above her head. The rider looked familiar, even though Petra was sure they'd never met before. Long hair golden and gleaming, the rider resembled someone from a medieval storybook, and Petra thought about Guinevere. The horse drew nearer, and the rider's features were in view now, and still Petra stood her ground, waiting. The horse was either going to ride by her or trample her, but she was unable to move now as last minute panic set in and she tried to run. The horse reared up in front of her, but the rider was completely confident in her saddle.

"Why are you not moving? Why don't you run? You are so stupid! You think you know better than me? I should have ridden over the top of your ugly head. James would not love you if your head was all caved in now would he? You have no right to him. He's mine, in this life and the next..." At this the rider leaned over the neck of her horse who was still panting and snorting with the recent exertion, and glared at her up close. Petra could see the colour of the rider's eyes – the depth of passion in them and smelled her very stale breath as she spat out her final words. "You don't belong here – GO AWAY or Die!!!"

With that Petra woke up with a start, panting with fear. She was hot, and the air in the small room felt dank and stale. The awful smell of the Rider's breath was still there. It felt as though it was on her skin, making it crawl. Scratching at her arms, Petra sprang out of bed, turning the light on and searched the sheets expecting to find ants or fleas to explain the feeling on her body. The sheets were clear, but damp from her sweat.

After a few deep breaths, and a stern word with herself about being overly imaginative, she convinced herself to climb back into bed and contemplate sleep again, leaving the light on in the room this time. At least an hour of tossing and turning, replaying the dream over in her mind, preceded a deep sleep that was interrupted by a knocking on her door. Four-thirty am and it was time to rise. Sleep deprivation making her foggy and slow, Petra climbed into her clothes and trudged to the meditation room. The dream stayed with her as she tried to relax into a meditation guided by the yogi.

As she worked her way through a delicious breakfast, the urge to break the silence imposed on her by the rules of the retreat waged war with her desire to see it through to the end, knowing she was now at the half way mark. She wanted desperately to seek the wise counsel of someone about her dream, but hesitated all through the day until finally the chance to do so evaporated into the sunset.

As she readied herself for bed that evening, she considered the wisdom of both leaving the light on and praying for safety in her sleep to one of the guardian angels she was sure assisted her through her daily life and decided on the latter. Sleep finally overcame her.

This time the feeling of knowing she was caught in a dream was not there, but the fear certainly was.

The Rider from the night before was this time standing firmly on the ground in front of a great lake, legs evenly spread, one hand on her hip, the other holding the mighty staff firmly in front of her. Her hair was blowing in the breeze and there were dark clouds gathering as though rain might start to fall heavily at any moment. An occasional flash of lightening burst through them in the distance adding to the drama of the confrontation about to come.

"So, you came back!" The rider threw it out as a challenge and waited for Petra to respond.

"Who are you? And what do you want from me?" Petra thought she knew, but the answer seemed too strange to believe. Alice was lying in a hospital bed two hundred miles away, so how could she be here? And how did she know about Petra anyway?

Besides, so far as Petra knew, Alice was a mousy blonde waif of a woman, not a powerful Amazon capable of looking like this and presenting as a strong kick-arse type who might have given Thor a good run for his money.

"You dare to ask? You who are so much the slut you would sleep with another woman's husband? You who would not even wait until her death to stake your claim? You dare to ask who I am?" She moved the staff to her other hand – the act serving to remind Petra of the power of the woman's presence somehow. "You are the one who has to GO AWAY and stop stealing another woman's husband. Or I will hunt you down and gut you like a fish. You must stop. You must atone for what you have done. And you must accept that James will *never* be yours."

At this, she turned and faced the lake, effectively dismissing Petra. Petra on the other hand had questions that had to be answered.

"Wait!"

The Rider paused, but did not turn around.

"I want to know something."

The Rider continued to stand still, her back to Petra, but hopefully listening and so Petra plunged on.

"If you are Alice, then you must know that James has been good to you and deserves to be happy. And if you are not Alice, but only a representative of hers, then you must know that I have not done anything wrong, but perhaps James is the one whom you should be speaking to."

At that, the Rider turned and strode across the short terrain to stand directly in front of Petra, so close that Petra could have counted the number of lashes beneath her eyes. Behind those eyes was darkness and it took everything she had to not take a step back in fear.

"You are responsible for this, so YOU are the one who should be the most afraid. I will NOT give James up, even after I'm gone. He's mine and YOU. CANNOT. HAVE. HIM! Be GONE!

With that she disappeared and the storm started to rain down upon Petra who turned and ran, suddenly absolutely terrified. The terror continued as she crashed her way through endless swamp, searching desperately for a way to gain solid ground. At every turn she was struck by branches, and at times sank deeply into mud. The stench was disgusting and she found as she tried to hold onto something solid that it was merely the dead carcass of a sheep whose flyblown fleece came away in her hands. Big plump wriggling maggots crawled over her hands in the slimy mess of the fleece and she tried to throw it as far away from her as possible. Unsuccessful at that, she plunged her hands into the mud and screaming turned in another direction only to find that she had sunk into the mud up to her arms, and she couldn't move. Sinking this time, she screamed and heard pounding hooves coming closer. Terrified that it was the Rider again, she stopped screaming and tried to hide. The pounding continued… and suddenly she was awake, and being shaken.

"Miss are you ok? Miss… Petra, wake up, are you ok?"

She focused on the face before her, finding it belonged to a kindly looking older man with a grey beard that matched the colour of his eyes. Confused she simply gulped a couple of times then nodded. "Sorry, bad dream," she managed to mutter then moved herself back onto her pillow and in so doing extracted herself from his grasp of her shoulders.

"Sorry to break into your room but we heard some screaming and you didn't answer when we knocked." The old man nodded in the direction of a younger man who simply nodded at her. Both were dressed in flowing robes and she remembered with a start that she was supposed to be in a *silent* retreat.

"Sorry, I was having a nightmare." Petra reached for the water in the glass beside her bed and took a gulp. "I think I'm supposed to be silent, but I do need to talk about my dream." And suddenly she burst into tears.

"My dear, it's ok. And maybe you do need to talk about this. It's nearly 4:30 am; do you want to come and talk to me after breakfast?" Petra nodded. "Ok, come and seek me out. Just ask for Faramin ok?"

Petra nodded again and put her glass back on the bedside table. Faramin stood up and with a glance indicated to the other man that they should leave now.

After breakfast, Petra went in search of the older man, but was told that no such person existed in the area. Asked to describe him, and his companion, several times simply resulted in shakes of the head and confusion so she stopped. With that she decided that the retreat was not delivering for her what she wanted and checked out early to return home.

CHAPTER 20

Petra had refused to talk to James for two days since her return from her Retreat, and James was becoming quite worried. The situation with Alice was also concerning him, but he knew that at least while she was in hospital nothing further could be done by him at this time. However, Petra was of considerably greater concern as it was unlike her to avoid him. She just was not that kind of person. If something was troubling her she was more likely to upset people by being very upfront about it than shying away from even difficult issues.

He decided to drive by her house and see if he could find out what was wrong. An uneasy feeling accompanied him to her front door and he rang the bell.

He knew she was home because her car was parked in front of the house, but she took an incredibly long time to answer the door. When she did, he was quite shocked at her appearance. Dark circles under her eyes told of sleeplessness and a complete lack of makeup was also highly unusual for her.

"Hello James," was all she said as she opened the door.

"Hi. I was worried, are you OK?"

With that she burst into tears and backed away into the room, leaving him to follow – or not.

Within a heartbeat he was beside her, holding her in his arms as she continued to sob. Scared of whatever it was making her this way, he had no choice but to wait and listen when she was ready to talk. When she finally told him about her nightmares that had continued all week, he was shocked.

"Oh my God sweetheart, I don't know what to say."

"I know, me too. I think I thought you would think I was just bat-shit crazy." She paused and went to the kitchen, returning in a moment with tissues and a glass of water.

"Not only is this relentlessly affecting my sleep, but during the day I feel like she's watching me, and I'm scared. I don't know what to do, but I don't want to antagonise her."

"I know. I mean…well, actually I don't know what to say."

"Well I have decided I don't want to be with you until she's at least died and gone. I don't know for sure if it's actually Alice who is affecting my dreams, but I do know for sure that if it is, and she's not even dead yet, that I don't want any part of this. I'm sorry, but I want you to go." Petra stifled a sob again as she said this last part. Clearly the decision had been made, and James could see no point in trying to dissuade her. But he was heartbroken.

Turning at the doorway, he wanted to let her know how he felt and to reassure her he was willing to wait.

"Petra, I love you, and want to be with you. I know that this is a difficult time, but it can't last and I really want you to know I'll be doing everything possible to be with you soon. Please call me if anything, at *any* time comes up and you need me ok? I just *love* you so much." He crossed the room quickly and took her in his arms. They were both crying as they parted, neither knowing how long their separation might last.

He made it to the car, and reversed into the street, taking off with a roar and parking up at a nearby park to sob out his feelings of frustration in peace.

Later that day he returned home and sat for a long time in his car, not really wanting to go inside to what had become no longer a home for him. The house was dark, and he knew Brett and Deanna were likely inside either getting dinner ready or watching TV, and he found it hard to face them in his current mood

Finally he decided to head next door to Dons and invite him to have a beer down at the local surf club. Don took one look at James and could see his friend was close to hitting a brick wall emotionally and called out to Mary he'd be back in an hour or so.

Talking things over with Don was good. James told him all about Petra and what had happened earlier that day and Don just simply listened, nodding occasionally, and letting James know he had sympathy for his difficult situation. When he finished pouring his heart out, James looked up at Don and asked, "What would you do next if you were me?"

Don took a long time to answer. "Buddy I have to say that I really can't even imagine what you are going through. I mean I've heard you, and understand the many layers and the dilemmas you're facing with Alice, and that's without the Petra factor added in. Man, I just don't know what to tell you my friend."

James finished his drink and stood up. "Yeah I'm hearing you. I don't know how I'd react if someone told me all this either. Some of it just sounds so far-fetched I can't comprehend it's actually happening to me. Come on – better get you home to your beautiful normal and totally lovely wife."

CHAPTER 21

James sat in front of his wife and watched her breathe. The machine was doing some of that for her, but he was mesmerised by her rising and falling chest.

He was warring with the words inside him and all that he wanted to say to her. She had made his life miserable for so long, and he could barely comprehend how much he now despised her, and all she had done to him. He tried to force his mind back to the early days of their marriage and how happy he had been, but struggled to get through the gatekeeper of his mind that was siding with the injustices of the last few years. Was it really possible that she had tried to set him – or Brett or her own daughter even – up for her murder? Was she really *that* deranged? How was that even be possible? Why had he not seen the *madness* creeping in before now?

Certain that she could not hear him anyway, he decided to vent his frustration about his life, her life, and her treachery to her as she slept. He had read many times about the potential for a comatose patient to actually be aware of what was going on about them, but decided that he no longer cared if she did in fact hear him. If he was lucky she would not leave the hospital again and would be now facing her final days. A part of him was very glad this was the case and while a remnant of the man who had once said 'I do' many years

106

earlier remained, the reality was that he could no longer endure the waiting.

"I can't believe you would go so far to hurt me. I don't know what you think I ever did to you that was so bad as to deserve this, but I'm flabbergasted at the lengths you seem to want to go to, to keep me."

Finding he could no longer sit, he got up and started pacing as he talked of all the frustrations and years of unhappiness in his marriage. After nearly two hours he was finally done. He'd cried, and raged, and talked, and even pleaded with Alice to let him go and find happiness, and for her to also let go and find her own peace beyond this life. At the end, he kissed her on the forehead and left the room. Bypassing the nurse's station, he made his way downstairs to his car and headed for the coast. Yearning for solitude and the beach he parked up and walked for the next two hours.

CHAPTER 22

Deanna's face was enough to spark fear into James's heart. She was angry – that much was clear. It appeared that her entire body might be exuding enough electrical current that it could have collectively run the national grid. Her teeth were clenched, and she could barely get the words out without spitting them.

"So – did you have a good time? Did ya?"

"Dee – what's going on?"

"As if you didn't know. What do you think I am, stupid? You dirty low life, fucking *bastard*!" She turned away and looked out the window, but was too upset to register the cars passing below, or the rolling storm clouds gathering in the distance. Fingers clenched, she desperately wanted a cigarette, but was unable to light up in the hospital.

"Actually Deanna, sorry but I have absolutely zero idea of what has upset you." James sighed and sank into the only chair in the room. He looked around at the starkly furnished room and wondered how anyone in here might ever feel even a smidgeon of empathy was considered when decorators were allocated their measly budget. For a hospital waiting room it was bereft of anything homely or warm. It was indeed just a room with a lousy view and a place to sit for a few minutes while their unwell friends or family were bathed, changed, or medicated.

"So what's up?" he asked when Deanna continued to stand rigidly with her back to him.

"I found mum's will in her room today."

"Yes, so?"

"She's signed over *everything* to you – I get *nothing*!" she hissed, spinning round to face him. "What the hell am I supposed to do when she finally dies? After all I've done for her – the Bitch! I can't believe it – you must have forced her to do it. And don't you dare lie to me, you bastard!"

"Dee, please, lower your voice – the entire hospital does not need to hear this."

"I don't care!" she yelled at him.

"Look, I do care. I'll not discuss this with you until you calm down." James looked at her hoping she might back down a little but could see she was in no mood to hear anything from him and left the room.

"Bastard!" she yelled after him as the door closed.

Deanna paced for a few moments before deciding to head outside to the smoker's garden. On her way downstairs the thought struck her. Was she sure that he hadn't tried to kill her mother? After all, he obviously had a lot to gain.

Brett found her a few minutes later, obviously having been sent to do so by James.

"Hey Lovely, are you ok?"

She snorted and took a long drag on her cigarette. He bummed a light from her and patiently smoked his own for a couple of minutes watching her.

"Look, it would be really helpful if you could at least talk to me – or are you also mad at me?"

Deanna glared at him, but decided it was worth at least airing her misery with a sympathetic ear. "Mum's will – I found it today and I've been cut out of it. So has Maddie." She stubbed out her cigarette and looked at him wondering how much to say of what was really on her mind. "James gets everything. I bet he knew that already, and I bet he had something to do with the state we found her in last week. You know, I always wondered about him."

As she spat forth her half-baked theories, Brett could only look at her and wonder what madness had overtaken his friend's stepdaughter.

"Dee…"

"Don't you dare 'Dee' me! I bet you are in on it. I bet you are both trying to kill my mother. I am going to have her body tested for everything possible when she does die you know. I read about husbands and wives killing each other all the time. A bit of arsenic over a few years and it's a slow painful death. It is exactly what Mum is going through."

"Deanna! I am shocked you could ever think such things about me, or James. We've stood by each other for so long through this now, there's no way we could ever think such things about each other. Surely you are kidding! What's gotten in to you?" Somewhere between angry and deeply hurt, Brett ran out of steam in his response to her allegations and decided to just leave her to finish venting alone. He ambled slowly back up to the ICU ward and wondered what to say to James. Deanna's tirade was the last thing he'd expected from her. What were they to do about it? He decided to leave that to his friend.

On entering the room where Alice lay breathing deeply with the help of thousands of dollars' worth of technical equipment, he noticed that James was wiping his eyes. He seemed to have done a

110

lot of that lately.   The stress of this was getting to all of them. God it was time for Alice to bloody well let go and GO, he thought as he took the chair beside James and sighed.

CHAPTER 23

"James, I need to see you."

Petra was unusually abrupt and he hesitated for a long moment before replying. "Ok. Um, are you ok?"

"Yes."

"Do you want me to come straight over?"

"Just as soon as you can please."

"Ok, I'll be there in about thirty minutes." She hung up before he could say more.

Arriving at her front door soon after, he was disturbed to find it open, and pushed it to enter. The first thing he noticed was the smell. Incense – overpowering and sickly sweet. Then he noticed the mess in the kitchen. Plates piled up in the sink, in a messy menagerie of crockery and silverware. Cold toast was popped up in the toaster, and butter was set out beside it. Ants were crawling everywhere having been attracted by an open jar of jam on the bench. He moved through the house calling out her name. Finding her in the bedroom, he was shocked by her appearance. She lay on the bed, pale and limp. Eyes moving as the rest of her body was still as death, taking in his appearance with something akin to gratitude, but he wasn't sure. Going quickly to her side, he took one of her hands in his and noticed how cold it was. "Petra, what the hell is going on? You look dreadful." He noticed a half full glass of water on the nightstand, and picked it up to check if it was fresh. It was vodka. She looked like she'd not slept or eaten in a week, and was very pale. The blue vein on the side of her neck stood out starkly against her white skin.

"I don't know what to do. Nothing works. I can't sleep, and I can't stay awake. I'm barely able to get up to go to the bathroom anymore. I had to open the door for you in case I fell asleep again before you arrived. I just can't stand it anymore James. Please help?" Her voice was soft as snow falling gently although she rushed all the words out as though fearful of losing them altogether. A very big wet tear rolled down her face towards her ear. He caught it and then pulled her towards him and held her tight.

Petra sobbed quietly for a few minutes.

He moved then and lay down beside her, and encouraged her to drop off and sleep for a while promising to be there while she slept. When she finally relaxed and her breathing was even, he got up and took another look around, quietly stacking the dishes into the dishwasher and setting it, and restoring the kitchen to order. Then he returned to her room and opened the window quietly to allow some air in, before lying down beside her again, taking her hand in his and calmly breathing himself into a very relaxed state. Whatever was going on, he could do nothing more until she'd rested and was able to talk to him about it.

Four hours later, he woke to find her looking at him with moist eyes. "Hey you," she whispered.

"Hey yourself." He moved to put his arm under her and draw her close. "So, what's going on baby?"

"I'm a little hungry – can you get some soup or toast maybe?" Petra looked like a small girl as she smiled over at him.

"Sure we can, are you ok to get up or do you want lunch in bed?" James looked at his watch and was surprised to see it was already mid-afternoon.

"I think I need to get up."

"Ok well you take your time ok - I'll go out to the kitchen and see what I can rustle up."

"Thank you." Petra lay back and watched him leave the room. Nervous about the conversation that lay ahead, she knew she was no longer able to deal with this problem alone and was very grateful for his having come straight to her.

A little while later she entered the kitchen to find him buttering toast and stirring a pot of scrambled eggs. "I couldn't find any soups so figured old fashioned eggs might be an ok alternative. Is that alright?"

Petra nodded and sat down smiling. James poured them both some juice, and put a plate of eggs and toast in front of her. "Now, no pressure, but sweetheart I really need to know what's been going on for you this last couple of weeks. I've been worried, but seeing you today was a shock and I need to know if you are ok?" He looked at her quizzically as she tucked into her eggs. After three mouthfuls she put down her fork and drained the glass of juice.

"Oh that was delicious. Thank you."

"Delaying tactics will not work Petra...I need to know what's going on." He reached for her hand and held it gently. Turning it over he kissed her palm, looking at her again, willing her to trust him enough to share everything that had happened.

Taking a deep breath, she started. First she told him the details of the dreams she'd had on retreat two weeks earlier. She apologised for having not been totally upfront about that, then moved on to explain that the intensity of those dreams was causing her to wake up fearing for her life every time she went to sleep.

"The images in my head are one thing, but it's the icy fear that courses through my body that is horrific. It's got to the stage where I'm terrified of falling asleep at all. And the worst part of it is that even if I do sleep, I don't rest at all because it feels like I'm fighting for my life even when I'm asleep. I tried drinking and that hasn't helped a lot either. I barely know what day it is, but I know I can't do this any longer. James, I'm terrified."

Tears fell as she talked, and she ignored them. Pausing finally, she wiped her face and reached for a tissue.

"And you are certain that Alice is somehow involved in this - what do you want to call it - this *campaign* against you? Do you know how crazy that sounds?"

"James, I'm sorry, but yes, and I'm sorry but I don't know what else to call it. She's disturbing me far more than anyone could if it was just dreams. I've had nightmares before, but this is different. And it's very real. I wake up feeling absolutely cold with terror."

James got up from the table and started pacing the kitchen. He was struggling to put this whole situation into any kind of order in his mind. What she was telling him seemed completely unreal, but he'd known Petra for years, and she could not have faked the way she was this morning. He also knew her to be sensible and calm, and definitely not given over to absurd fancies of the imagination.

"Ok, here's what we're going to do." He'd reached a decision so quickly that he'd barely even formed it properly before blurting it out. "Pack a bag, I'm taking to you to a hotel for the next few nights, until we sort this out. Maybe it's not about where you are, but at least I can be there with you, and sleep with you and somehow protect you."

"But James, if this *is* Alice torturing me in my sleep, the only reason she'd do that is because she thinks I'm after her husband, and for whatever bizarre reasons, and regardless of whatever we've done or not, she'll see this as a much greater issue... Won't' she?"

Petra was confused to even hear herself say the words out loud. When she'd told James earlier about what was going on in her sleep, she'd barely believed it herself, despite having come up with no alternative suggestions for what was disturbing her so profoundly. Now, the words had fallen from her mouth, she had trouble believing them herself.

" Petra, sweetheart, I can't think of any other options for now. At least if I'm with you, you might be less afraid when you wake up. And you can't keep going on the way you have been this last week."

"But we can't just sleep in a hotel for however long this is going to last. Actually, what is the latest? How is Alice?"

As James filled her in on all that had been going on for him, she went through the motions of putting an overnight back together, and then had a quick shower and dressed. They left the house as soon as possible, and drove to the Sheraton hotel near the hospital.

"I want to be with you as much as possible. But I do also have to spend some time at the hospital. I know you understand that." He leaned over and gave her a warm kiss on the cheek before getting out of the car. He'd booked a suite while she was showering and they were quickly checked in and observing the view from their fourth floor balcony.

"I know you prefer not to be too high off the ground, so I figured the fourth floor would be ok, but still afford a bit of a view. Is that ok?"

Petra laughed and moved closer to him, resting into his arms as he held her tight and kissed the top of her head. God she felt so good. To hell with Alice, he thought.

116

CHAPTER 24

Alice's body was slowly… ever so slowly… shutting down. Her breathing was shallow, the machines she was hooked up to doing most of the work now. People came and went from her room, some stayed a while to talk, hold her hand, and then kiss her forehead or touch her hair. Brett found that any more than five minutes was too hard to bear and left quickly each day. But the very thought of missing a visit tied him up in knots and so he tried hard to ensure he was consistently there at 10 am every morning. Deanna sat and read beside her bed for hours on end, occasionally stopping to look over at her mother and wonder what might have been going through her mind at various times over the past few years.

James had not been to see Alice for four days.

After finding Petra and bringing her to the hotel across from the hospital he decided he could hardly stand to be near Alice and finally forced himself to visit twice in the days immediately after 'rescuing' her, but had since decided that he was done! The fact that he'd broken his vows, and fallen head over heels in love with a woman other than his wife did not help his state of mind. He was also terrified that if he was left alone with Alice he might be tempted to do a number of things that would be ill received by anyone else.

He was also worried that he may just give into a strong desire to rant at her and tell her every horrible thing inside his mind. About how he felt about her and did not wish to add any fuel at all to her apparently venomous attacks on Petra. Unsure how he actually felt about that issue, he continued to push it from his mind, but it frequently flared up like a savage dog. Petra had continued to sleep fitfully in his arms at night, but was at least eating and sleeping better than she had been. He struggled deeply with his physical need for her - they'd both agreed to abstain from any sexual intimacy for the time being - but managed to calm himself enough to also get some sleep each night. Waking with aching balls every morning was torture, but he hoped that this whole situation might soon be resolved, and told himself every day that Petra was worth waiting for.

Deanna looked up as he entered the room, and scowled at him. She'd not spoken to him at all since her outburst last week and the tension lay heavily between them. More to worry about later, James told himself as he closed the door and took the four steps across the room to bring him to Alice's bedside.

"Any change?" he asked Deanna, hoping for a reasonable reply, but she carefully ignored him.

The machines beeped and sighed for a full minute, then Deanna raised her head and looked at him. "Where have you been? You've not been here for days? Why do you even care?" Her voice lowered to a hissed whisper as she poured forth her frustration at him. "What do you want from her? Can't you see she's dying now? You must be so pleased!"

"Deanna, please, can we talk about this?"

"Why?"

"Because you have it all wrong!"

Deanna paused for a moment, doubt clearly causing her to hesitate before speaking further. "Outside!" She jerked her head at the door and quickly left the room. He caught up with her striding fast towards the elevators. Several other people were milling about waiting for the doors to open so they both stepped in and ignored each other until they reached the ground floor. Deanna headed to the smokers' garden and lit up. "You have two minutes!" She glared at him, trying to look as menacing as possible, but failing miserably. He realised how scared and vulnerable she must be feeling and decided to put the animosity of the previous week to one side.

"Alice's will has a whole section added to it that does concern you. And Deanna, I would never ever see you out of pocket. You've been like a daughter to me for many years now, and despite how hard these last few years have been between Alice and me, you are someone we both love very much."

He could see her softening slightly and continued, hoping he could resolve all her concerns before they returned to the room upstairs. "Alice and I decided years ago that if anything happened to the other, our wills would reflect that our estates would pass to the other, and then once both of us died the balance would then go to you and Maddie equally. However, in the interim, to ensure you are not out of pocket, you get to take anything you want of your Mum's personal effects, and of course, I'll see you are well set up in your own home if that's what you want. I'd never see you out on the street or feeling hard done by. You have to believe that."

By the time she put her butt into the ashtray, Deanna was almost smiling with relief. "Oh, I'm so sorry I thought those things of you – I know you could not really have hurt Mum. But well, you can see how I thought..." her voice trailed off and she shrugged, finding the words she wanted were out of reach. "Where have you been this week?"

James hesitated, not quite sure what to tell her. After the previous discussion he was concerned that anything putting him in a bad light with her would resurrect any remaining resentment. "Well, I just needed a break you know? I mean, it's been a bloody tough few weeks and I really don't think my being here or not makes any difference at all to Alice. In fact, maybe it makes it worse. I don't know. It's just a hard time that's all. You know, it's been twenty-seven years since I last smoked, but I've craved a cigarette a lot lately. Would you mind?"

"No, no way. Don't you dare start smoking again! It's too hard to quit"

James must have looked surprised and annoyed, and so Deanne relented and held out her packet. He took a cigarette and flicked the lighter she offered, took two puffs and coughed. "Oh my God that's awful!" She took it off him and smoked it herself, laughing at him.

"Serves you right old man."

"Yeah well, at least the craving might stop now. I think I'll stick to chocolate!"

Companionably they wandered back into the building a few minutes later and found Brett in Alice's room, sobbing.

"Oh, I was so worried. I had this awful dream about Alice last night and… oh it was just awful. I thought she was dead already but she had turned into this witch with scrawny fingers and… oh I just… don't know how to describe it really."

He wiped his eyes as Deanna gave him a quick hug. When Brett looked up at James, his friend had turned as pale as Alice's sheets.

CHAPTER 25

"The doctors say it will be any day now. That's good right? I so wish this could just be over. I can't believe how much she's holding on", said James in despair

Alice had taken a turn in the night and was increasingly a mere shadow of her former self. James found it hard to believe she had aged so much in such a short period of time. He looked out at the ocean scene before him, enjoying the view from the balcony of the Sheraton.

"You know I could easily get used to this. Maybe I'll sell the house and we'll get an apartment here on the beach... would you like that?" Petra raised her head and they kissed briefly.

The nightmares were continuing, but Petra was at least able to snatch some sleep and rested as much as possible between times. With James's help, she was also eating moderately well and they made time every day to walk for half an hour along the waterfront. However, the nightmares were taking a particularly savage turn now, and neither of them wanted to confront the ugly truth that they were going to need some help, and maybe that would be of a psychological nature.

"I need to tell you about the dream from last night. I also want to get out of here and some fresh air ok? How about a walk down to the garden?" Petra moved away from his embrace as she spoke, and he could see she was struggling emotionally to sound and look normal. He was growing to know her better every day and sensing her moods was becoming second nature to him now.

"Sure – I'll just make a quick call ok?"

A few minutes later they were sitting quietly in the hotel garden, facing the ocean. Another couple was seated nearby, minding their own business, drinking coffee. The man was reading the newspaper and his companion appeared to be simply staring out to sea.

"So, last night, when I woke up, I was bathed in sweat, and could not seem to remember where I was at first. The feeling of cold terror was awful, again, so much so that I am almost getting used to it. I just wish the dreams would stop."

"I know we talked about sleeping pills, and I agree that you might find yourself trapped in the sleep instead of able to actually wake yourself up, but are you sure you don't want to at least try? Maybe take a half tablet?" suggested James.

"No, getting to sleep is not the problem. And I now drop off knowing that the outcome will be the same, so I'm not even so bothered by that any more. I do however wish I could find some sense in the events of the dreams," replied Petra.

"Tell me about last night then." James tightened his arm around her, and kissed the top of her head.

Petra had found herself in a swamp, where warm gases erupted around her feet everywhere. It was dark, but there were red glows coming from fires burning in the distance. She wanted to move in any direction, as a sense of urgency overtook her. As she stepped to the right, the very earth seemed to growl at her. A rumbling deep underground started as she moved, so she returned to the standing position she'd started in. Deciding to try another direction, she experienced the same reaction from whatever was under her feet.

All attempts to move from a standing position elicited the same response and finally she looked up, seeking an escape there. Above her the sky was crisscrossed with dark beams. She could see the stars, but wondered if she was actually standing inside a very old, exceptionally large shipwreck or church. Bats flew about from side to side of the structure, eliciting squealing noises as they went. At times, she could feel the breeze they stirred up in her hair and shuddered.

A deepening roar like a distant tsunami increased in volume, and the earth began to shudder. Petra strained her eyes into the darkness above and to the sides, seeking any clue as to how to move away and seek shelter from whatever was coming. Instead as the sound grew, she found herself standing even straighter, paralysed with fear, like a lightning rod stuck rigid, but glowing with energy. Then she saw the warrior - as she now thought of her - moving, gliding above the ground towards her. Her hair was wilder than her eyes, and her breasts heaved with passion as she came closer and closer until finally she was only inches away from Petra. Petra could smell the foul breath of her opponent and gasped. The warrior rewarded her reaction with laughter.

"You are stuck now aren't you? How does that feel? Are you frightened? Are you ready to fight for your life? Are you ready to fight for your *love*? What is it you really want my dear? You don't think for a moment I was ever going to make it easy for you do you? Foolish of you if you did!

The singsong voice bantered, threatened, and taunted, and yet the warrior's lips never moved. Petra's skin crawled as she tried to not show the deep fear that held her still in front of this 'woman' who had now been chasing her through her sleep for several weeks. Was it Alice? She was still not quite sure. It seemed that Alice was somehow involved, and yet this 'thing' did not look like her. How was she able to bring this to a conclusion?

"What do you want from me!?" Petra finally screamed – or at least she tried to. Her voice came out of her body weak and thready. She tried again to inject some passion into it, and again failed. The warrior laughed at her. Suddenly Petra found her voice; "What have I done to you? WHO the fuck are you? Leave me ALONE!" Finally Petra felt the resonance in her words. "Why don't you FUCK OFF!!!"

She woke up suddenly then, the sound of the warrior's laughter still pervading her senses, feeling cold and disoriented. The dreams were so real.

"And when I woke up, it was as though the warrior was in this very room. I could hear her laughter even though I was sort of awake. I still have no bloody idea what this is about, and yet I still feel certain that Alice is somehow part of this."

A silent tear had escaped her eye as she finished speaking. James leaned over and kissed it from her face. "Sweetheart, I think we need to get some help with this. It's getting to be such an ongoing issue, that I don't see how we can continue to deal with it alone."

"Yes but what if a doctor or shrink just thinks I'm a nut job. I don't want to be medicated and counselled to the nth degree every Tuesday afternoon for an hour. That could also take months to start reaching any kind of solution. And, maybe this will all stop once Alice has actually died. I get a strong sense every day that she is somehow involved, even though I am not quite sure how. So – let's just wait a few more days ok?"

"Honey I hear you, but my concern is that if Alice is involved in these night terrors somehow, then there's a chance isn't there that her being dead might even escalate them? I've been doing a bit of research, and earth bound bodies, spirits, poltergeists, and even astral travel all seem to point to some of what's going on here, I just don't want to take any chances that we miss an opportunity to actually deal with this properly."

James felt funny saying the words, but had been thinking for a few days now that maybe there was in fact some kind of evil spiritual connection between Alice and Petra. What or how, he was unable to even begin to imagine, but he did know that the timing and the toxicity of the whole situation was a little too coincidental for him to dismiss the fanciful ideas he had started to read about.

"Excuse me, but can I offer you some help?"

They both looked over at the woman sitting nearby. Her husband had gone inside, and she was sitting quietly, leaning anxiously towards them, the wind rustling through her luxurious thick grey hair.

Mynda had been listening intently to the couple talking about terrible nightmares and the possibility of there being some kind of spiritual issues and finally decided to introduce herself.

Having been a medium and counselling spiritual worker for most of her life, she was aware that there was no coincidence in the timing of her sitting outside with her husband Terry at that moment. She'd felt drawn to do so despite the not very warm afternoon.

CHAPTER 26

"Here she is; Hashihime, the Japanese maiden who was spurned by her lover, and ended up being turned into an 'Oni' when jealous rage overtook her. It is said that she transcends life, and took on the powers of the devil while still alive. It is said that her spirit has evolved throughout the years so that she is now able to assist the troubled lovers who are treated badly by their husbands."

"The clue that had me wondering if it was her, was that you mentioned being stuck on land surrounded by water. Given that your wife is still alive James, I am sure that somehow she must have taken on the help of Hashihime while she is still here. The big question of course, is what will likely happen after she dies?"

James and Petra looked at each other silently. It all just seemed so bizarre. Was someone waiting behind the door on the right to jump out and say 'Jokes on you!'? They had talked for hours the night before with Mynda and her husband Terry about what had been happening in their lives. Mynda was immediately warm and empathetic, but troubled by their story. Finally as it neared eight o'clock, she promised to look into some of the things that came to mind and resume their discussion as soon as possible.

This morning she had called and invited them to breakfast.

126

Looking triumphantly at her guests, she waited for a reaction. The waiter finally arrived to break the silence and offered them coffee or tea. The welcome distraction gave everyone time to collect their own thoughts, and James was the first to speak.

"Mynda, this is all just a… well. What I'm trying to say is that… Well this is just *insane!*"

He looked helplessly at Petra hoping for some flash of normality to burst forth from her, but her shoulders had slumped, and she was listlessly stirring her tea. He took her hand and squeezed it, as one giant tear escaped her tired eyes. "Mynda, thanks, this is helpful I suppose, but it just seems so… so… mad!"

Mynda smiled in sympathy at James. "I know this seems hard to take in, but it is the only thing that makes sense. And – the best part is, that if we know what we're dealing with, we can deal with it! Right?" She had become used to unusual spiritual events in the lives of those around her over the years, but knew that this was potentially an exceptionally interesting situation. She nodded at him, trying to encourage him to do the same and to really hear what she was trying to say. Petra had resumed stirring her tea, wiped her face, and looked completely shattered.

"What was the dream last night?" Mynda asked.

"I don't want to talk about it. It was just too horrible," she replied.

"That's ok, I understand." Mynda went on. "Look, I know this is a strange situation, but let's recap a few things ok? Alice has had years of lying about, being 'unwell', and yet you know that she has been sneaky, and cunning in some of her odd behaviour. Before that she was once kindness personified, but grew into a shrewish wife who didn't care for much of anything or anyone. She always wanted more than anyone was able to give her in terms of affection and the result of that was that she disengaged fully from relationships. Am I right so far?"

James nodded.

Mynda continued. "The worst part of her behaviour was usually centred on her need to keep you constantly by her side, and to control you."

James nodded again. He was feeling decidedly uncomfortable for having shared so much of his personal life with this stranger, regardless of how helpful she was trying to be. He took in her thick grey hair, cut to a long bob shaping an aging beautiful face that was both gentle and strong. Her elegant hands featured long fingers with several silver rings on each, all Celtic in design, some set with cabochon gemstones. Her hazel eyes were fringed with dark grey lashes, and framed with perfectly shaped brows and when she talked, her hands punctuated every expression, while her brows ran marathons. And yet she was so compelling in her presence. Far from being a 'regular' older lady, he knew instinctively that she was wise and true. Her ability to help them was real – he could just feel it. In that same way, he could feel that Petra was losing her fight to keep up with it all and was growing increasingly tired and despondent with each passing day.

James decided that he'd better pay attention and put his doubts aside. Picking up his cup, he drank some coffee and then spoke. "Mynda, I don't know how we are going to get through this next few days, but I am worried about Petra, and hope that what you are saying is right. But if you are, then I get the feeling that the danger to her life is very real. What can we do?"

Mynda smiled at him. "We'll get through this together, I promise. Now, can you please get home sometime this morning and see if you can find anything at all that Alice may have hidden away, that indicates any interest in Japanese mythology. Let's make certain of what we're dealing with. For now it's just a very strong likelihood that it is Hashihime – but I'd like to be sure."

Hell Hath No Fury

CHAPTER 27

Alice wandered about in her mind, oblivious to anyone watching her, and their physical comings and goings. Her entire being was focused on everything happening around her internally – her real world was now fully that of the mind. She was unaware of the machines assisting her to breathe, and didn't care about the drugs running through her body. She felt powerful, alive, and capable of anything.

Alice had spent a long time learning to be still, to move through her home, the lives of those around her, and even those people she did not count as close friends. She could visit her neighbours – and often did. She wondered if Mary really was ok with Don's pornography collection – and his personal need to wear her bra and panties when he masturbated. Or how secretive Mary was in relation to her shopping. Victoria's Secret was well patronised by Mary, and yet despite their joint passion for silky undergarments, Alice never actually saw them wearing such items in front of each other. Maybe Mary had a lover?

Alice soon grew bored with their silly life, and moved on to sometimes watch her daughter. Deanna would have been horrified to see her mother observing her drug use. And the occasional man and woman she visited paid for three-way sex when they all got high and fucked like rabbits for hours on end. Part of her was fascinated by the whole thing, but also equally repulsed by the knowledge that this was her daughter's way of enjoying herself.

Then there was Brett, and his almost daily forays to the underworld of the gay lifestyle at The Den downtown. There he would drink, and take part in quick casual sex with tradesmen seeking a thrill instead of lunch, where glory holes were *tres du jour* so that no one knew who was blowing who. Alice found this entire cesspit fascinating. Who knew that such places existed, or were frequented by such interesting people? Men of all ages, many of whom were straight but intensely curious and addicted to their dark side being explored by strangers, or transsexuals needing to fill a physical need and unsure where else to get it. Men who were lonely because they were stuck in marriages of 'normality' but inside desperately in need of a man's touch. Yes, Alice was deeply cynical of this place and all who played there, but she was also curious about the players and so frequently stopped by.

But her favourite place to be was with Petra. Petra had become her nemesis. The one person she hated the most, and was enjoying tormenting her in this process of stripping her of her sanity. It was a careful, easy, studied process, and she was determined to win. For a start, Petra had no idea of who she was dealing with. Alice was slowly becoming someone else. She could feel it. Never before had she desired, and enjoyed, such power. All her life she'd wanted to be significant, and now finally, she felt that level of importance surging through her. She was someone to be reckoned with now. She knew that whether she was visiting her neighbours, or Brett's playground, she could if she chose to, simply whisper in the ears of those she picked on to make them feel intensely uncomfortable. But while that was a lot of fun, Petra was even more so.

With Petra, she could make her wish she could just curl up in desperate need for sleep and want to die. She could make her sleep so disturbed that she'd be terrified of death. And she could control her mood with doubts about everything she was and felt, with barely more effort than snapping her fingers.

And Petra, after all, deserved to be taught a lesson. James did too, but he could wait for now. Alice was enjoying the games with Petra far too much to worry about James yet.

Over the years of being unwell Alice had filled her time reading books, and when her daughter gave her an iPad set up with kindle on it she reverted to reading books that no one else even knew were of interest to her. She would read, then Google and study things, people, events, and history until her sharp mind was able to move swiftly across a wide range of subjects. The ones that held the most fascination for her were historical figures across various cultures. Fascinated by tales of women wounded and betrayed by lovers; cads who callously disregarded the women who sought only to pleasure them. Women who sacrificed themselves for lost love. One such demon was Hashihime – the goddess of the bridge.

Legend had it that Hashihime was spurned by her husband for a younger woman, and so enraged with jealousy was she that she vowed to get revenge even if it meant losing her own life in the process. She wept at the Uji Bridge and begged the gods to turn her into a demon so that she could avenge herself. The gods finally relented and agreed to turn her into a demon if she would spend twenty-one nights immersed in the river. She did this and returned from the underworld to attach herself to her former husband and his mistress at night through their dreams, only to be thwarted by his having sought help to do so using white magic. Hashihime was so upset that she swore to return and finish her task on behalf of all women who were spurned.

Now it's fair to say that demons and goddesses are highly speculative ideas for many people, but it is also true that black magic and dark arts do exist. For Alice, this idea became an obsession over her time of being bedridden. She had always studied meditation as a younger woman, and even dabbled in Buddhist teachings for a while.

Learning to harness the power of her mind, which had very little else to occupy it over several years other than concern as to the daily whereabouts of her husband, had served her well. Just as any shaman, mystic, light worker or psychic can learn to do, she was proficient at astral travel and very deep levels of meditation.

The difference was that Alice was not remotely interested in the good energy and helpfulness of light workers – she was instead focused on getting satisfaction for all the wrongs she'd been subjected to all her life. Men were the reason she was unhappy – everything in her life that was good, bad or a waste of time always came back to her problems with men. She had been troubled by men's filthy hands since she was a shy young girl just starting to sprout into womanhood. Being forced to have sex with her cousin at the age of fourteen, was followed by several boyfriends who thought she was easy and treated her like a commodity. She felt that her first husband had thought of marriage as a marginally better economic alternative to white slavery. When that marriage ended there were other men who frequented her life for a few years, but they were not much better. By the time she met James she was tired, nearly broken with defeat over how her body was used by selfish uncaring lovers. Love eluded her but danced tantalisingly close with each encounter – most men in her life had started with the promise of love, but soon changed, and she became further disillusioned by its ideals.

James was different. He'd seen her as needing to be rescued and his own lack of success with love lent an additional level of desperation to his search for someone he could take care of. They fitted each other's needs perfectly at the time, and for several years enjoyed great happiness together. Both committed to their 'happy ever after' story, and neither imagined that the intensity could so easily burn out and leave them wanting more. Alice became suspicious when James travelled away for work and he in turn became defensive when closely questioned about his time spent away from home. The more he tried to convince her he was faithful, the more she disbelieved him.

The irony was that he was so terrified of the consequences of her finding him unfaithful that he avoided other women like the plague. Too many of his friends had lost so much in the divorce courts that it just became a non-option for him. The wedges between them expanded and split them apart until neither really knew how to communicate their desire to return to their happy filled early days. So the seeds of destruction in their marriage grew like Jack's beanstalk, higher and bolder, piercing their cloud nine forever.

*

The doctor checked the chart, and wrote something down before sternly looking at Brett. "You are family I take it?"

"Yes, sort of!" Brett suddenly felt very uncomfortable under the doctor's gaze.

"Well, you'd best get the rest of Mrs Strong's family in, she's fading now, and we need to have a serious discussion about the next steps in her care." He looked at his watch, then murmured something quietly to the assistant at his side, before turning back to Brett. "I'll be back at 2 pm sharp."

Without waiting for any acknowledgement from Brett, the doctor turned and left the room, his assistant trailing silently behind him. Brett looked at Alice for a long moment and said a silent prayer for this to be the end, and left to call James and Deanne.

Two hours later they were all ushered into the small office next to the nurse's station. Doctor Fredrickson didn't waste time on niceties. "Mrs Strong is fading, and will soon be unable to breathe on her own. I've seen these situations where family does everything to keep their loved ones alive for a long as inhumanly possible and other times where the family is resigned to the final steps in the journey. I'm sure you're all aware that Mrs Strong will not be able to make any permanent recovery from this point forward – it is now a matter of time before she…" he paused to clear his throat, "passes away. I'm very sorry for your loss. Now – I require agreement and instructions from you," he directed a steady look at James, indicating his understanding of James' role as Alice's next of kin "regarding the next few hours of her care." He cleared his throat again, perhaps for dramatic effect, thought Deanne.

"How long do you think it may be?" James was mindful of his wife's incredible capacity for holding on, and was hopeful that he didn't sound too eager for the end as he asked the question.

"I'd say it will be up to forty-eight hours at this stage." Dr Fredrickson glanced briefly from James to Brett and Deanna, wondering for a moment about the relationships between the three of them, then decided as he usually did, that he really didn't care that much to know. All his patients were temporary. By the time he became involved in their cases, they were well past being people he could get to know and their families were simply extras in the scene being played out each day on his stage. He'd decided many years ago that learning too much about the dying only made it harder for him to sleep at night, and so he carefully closed himself off from forming personal relationships with anyone other than his colleagues and family.

He shuffled his papers, pausing with his pen held above the documents in front of him, and returned his gaze expectedly upon James. Husbands were usually a lot more volatile emotionally than wives were at the end, he'd observed. All that keeping it deep inside, stiff upper lip and so on. 'Don't cry if you're a man…' humpf! What rubbish he'd always thought. If someone you loved was dying, let it out and stop being such a martyr. But this husband was different. James Strong seemed very resigned to the inevitable. He mentally shook the thoughts from his head and returned to the job at hand.

"No heroics Doctor. We're all ready for this to be over in a natural way, without fuss." James sounded as steady as he looked.

Dr Fredrickson made his notes, thanked them for coming to the meeting, and prepared to leave.

"Just one thing, it may last beyond the expected time, if there are any other family members who wish to come and say their goodbyes, now is the time to do that. I'll have Jeannie here liaise with you all if anything comes up that needs my attention. You can reach me via her." Jeannie nodded quietly and then followed the doctor from the room.

"Well that's that then… it's nearly over." Brett's voice wobbled noticeably as he spoke. He didn't like being in the hospital, or dealing with death and dying, but he certainly had had enough of the drama and its lengthy process. At odds with his feelings about that were the memories of the good times he'd had over the earlier years with Alice when she was pleasant to be around, and he thought he might still really miss her.

Deanna came up to him and wrapped her arms about him both seeking and giving support. James quietly left the room and went to stand beside Alice's bed. Looking down at her, he played over in his mind the last three years and wondered at the waste of all their time. He wondered how he might have felt if she had died quickly back then. Perhaps no differently than he did now. After all, he had been ready to leave her before her diagnosis, and only stayed to be supportive at the end. How could any of them have ever imagined it would take so long for the final curtain to fall?

He took her hand and held it for a moment, before putting it back on the bed and turning away. The tears in his eyes noted by the nurse entering the room as he left it were more for the time wasted in his own life than for the passing of his wife, but she was not to know that.

Hell Hath No Fury

CHAPTER 28

Doctor Yuki Masimoto found his way to the baggage hall, and out to the sunshine of Brisbane easily enough, but had somehow walked right past Mynda and James who were waiting for him inside. At seventy-six years of age, he refused to believe that his eyesight was less than perfect, and conveniently forgot to update his glasses prescription every year. Upright, and walking tall, he paused, took off his cream suit jacket and loosened his tie to match the style of several other warm travellers nearby. A pleasant younger man walked up to him holding a sign in his hand with his name on it in bold black letters, and he realised his mistake. James introduced himself and Mynda and soon they were on their way to Southport beach. It was a good time to get to know James better and the Doctor was delighted to find him calm, loaded with common sense, and most of all, fiercely in love with Petra. That would make this a lot easier.

He'd received the call from a colleague tracked down by Mynda who had Google searched for anyone with expertise and knowledge about Hashehemi. As a professor of Japanese legends, Doctor Masimoto had a particular fondness for the legends of the demons and gods of the underworld. When his colleague sent an email from a woman in Australia, with a few details he was intrigued. A lengthy phone call clarified exactly what they were concerned about and for the Professor the chance to observe the situation close up was too good to pass up and he was on a flight to Australia within hours.

When they arrived at the Sheraton Hotel where Petra was waiting, he was shocked to see how grey she looked. Unsure of her normal appearance, it was not hard to see that she was beautiful under the lank hair and sallow complexion. Huddled in a woolly jumper that was several sizes too big for her, despite the warmth of the day, she extended her hand and looked as though she really would have preferred a hug than a handshake, but he simply held her hand in both of his for a moment and made a small bow.

"It is very good to meet you Petra. I hope I can be of some help today."

"Dr Masimoto I'm so relieved, and excited that you are here."

"Please call me Yuki." He smiled and then addressed all three of them. "I've lived most of my life in the USA, so am completely used to western culture. May I have some water please, and a bathroom?"

Fifteen minutes later they were all sitting around the table in Petra's room, discussing the issue of Alice and what was happening to her mind and body now that she was actually dying.

Yuki began slowly. "What we don't know is whether her mind as Hashihime will continue to function in the after-world when Alice dies. I've done a lot of study about such things, and yet still we have no way of knowing about this. If she dies, and Hashihime dies 'in Alice' at the same time, then that is good. Petra will be free of Hashihime's influence. But my real concern is that if that does not happen, then the alternative will be that Alice will die, and Hashihime will actually be stuck in the spirit of Alice and this entire situation may continue and even escalate. If we can exorcise Hashihime from Alice before Alice dies, then that is my best recommendation."

Everyone nodded their heads, trying to be sure of understanding Yuki's words. It all sounded so complex and more than a little sureal.

"Can you get me in to see Alice please James?"

"Yes of course. When would you like to go?"

"Immediately. There is no time to waste."

On the way to the hospital, James pondered exactly what to make of this bizarre situation. Not for the first time, his feelings of utter helplessness momentarily overwhelmed him. "Yuki, is there anything I could have done differently to prevent this?"

"Young man, I doubt there is anything you could have done. My understanding is that these spirits that attach themselves to those among us are often waiting for a chance to be invited by someone who already has some big issues that never got sorted out on the therapist's sofa. From what you've told me about Alice, this is likely a similar situation. Don't worry about 'what ifs', you'll only drive yourself mad." He chuckled and wiped his brow for the twentieth time on a large white handkerchief. "My word it is very warm here." He went on to say that one mad person in any family was more than enough.

"Amen to that Yuki. Amen to that!"

James thought for a moment before asking what was really bothering him. Then decided to plunge in anyway. "Yuki, if you don't mind my asking, what makes you so interested in this?"

"Well I have always been interested in legends and mythology, but when I was a little younger than you, I saw first-hand how destructive a bad spirit can be to someone they latch on to. My brother was always a thrill seeker, but after his son died from an unexpected illness, he became increasingly unhappy, and one day I visited him and found he had started practicing dark magic. He was possessed in a way that made me not recognise him. I had studied already the ways of the old ones, but never had I expected to see something like that manifested into my own brother. Sumi was a gentle caring husband and father, but my sister in law was afraid to go to sleep because he was awake all night chanting and calling on the spirits to help him go into the darkest of places."

Yuki sighed, remembering that awful time, and went silent for a few moments. James finally said, "That sounds awful. What happened to him?"

"I knew someone at the university who did basically what I do now. Someone who travelled and sought knowledge on how to exorcise bad spirits, and I called him to ask for his help. He came and visited with my brother, and over several weeks spend a lot of time with him, urging the dark spirits to leave. It worked, up to a point. My brother was eventually able to sleep and started to get treatment for his grief, but his wife left him and very soon after e got sick and died. He simply gave up on living."

"Oh, I'm sorry to hear that."

"It was a long time ago now. I'll see him again one day." He grinned at James as they found a carpark and walked inside the hospital. "So you see I decided to study under Doctor Norikimo to learn what I could from him and was ready to take over doing this work before he died about twenty-six years ago."

James smiled at his guest, and thought of a hundred more questions, but they reached Alice's floor and it was time to get to 'work'.

CHAPTER 29

As they stepped inside Alice's room, James noted how much more shallow her breathing had become since that morning. 'It can't be long now', he thought, 'but hold on until we get this demon out of you ok?' He wasn't sure that could be called a silent prayer exactly, but he repeated it quietly and hoped it might help.

Yuki began by walking up to Alice and holding her hand, silently standing beside her with head bowed, moving his lips soundlessly. This lasted for nearly five minutes, and James almost wondered if the old man had fallen asleep standing, when Yuki released Alice and stepped back from the bed. He bowed low towards her then backed out of the room. James looked at Alice to see if there was any change at all, and nodding to the nurse sitting beside the bed, followed Yuki out into the hall. He found him sitting in a chair in the hallway, breathing deeply with his eyes closed, looking peaceful but for the hint of a frown knitting his eyebrows.

James sat beside him and waited quietly. Finally Yuki opened his eyes and looked at James with a twinkle in his eye. "We're in business my friend" he said with a smile. "I know how to deal with this problem. But we need to move quickly. I will need to spend some more time with Alice, and I'd prefer to do this without the nurse in there watching my work. I have found that sometimes

142

people don't understand what I do and it can be disruptive to be watched by skeptics. Can you arrange for you and me to have some time alone with her?"

"I'm sure I can, let me just think this through for a moment." James was not really sure how he'd be able to do this at all. It was pretty standard now for a medical nurse to be by Alice's side constantly. His request to be alone with her might raise some eyebrows. What if they thought he meant to through a pillow over her face." He grimaced at the memory of finding her that way only a few weeks, or was it days, earlier. God it seemed like months.

He decided anything was worth a try and so went and talked to the head nurse on duty and discussed with her the fact that he and his wife's spiritual teacher wanted to spend some time praying over her body and that Dr Masimoto had made a special trip to visit with her at this critical and sad time. Would it therefore be unseemly to have some private time with her to do this? To his surprise Nurse Morris was very understanding and within a few minutes, the room was cleared, and he and Yuki were standing on either side of her bed, each holding a hand.

As Alice breathed quietly and at times scarcely at all it seemed, Yuki indicated to James that he wanted him to continue holding her hand, and at all times remain calm, regardless of what came to pass. He'd already explained to him before they entered the room that he was going to try again to meet with Alice in spirit and he expected to meet the 'real' Alice, as well as Hashihime. From there, he would gauge how things were between them and work out what to actually do. "There is no guarantee of success of course, I have no firm idea of what may happen, but I'll do everything I can to make this all work out ok."

James only nodded, again questioning himself about the strange life he seemed to be leading lately.

As Yuki started to breathe deeply, he closed his eyes, and allowed himself to enter the world of the spiritual realm via a particularly deep meditation he'd developed over many years.   He asked first for protection from evil, and that his guides and teachers follow him and work with him to achieve learning and to bring love to the situation he was attempting to work through.   As he walked into what felt at first like a heavily wooded area, overgrown with bush and vines, he began to get a sense of lightness inside him and acknowledged and thanked his guides for joining him.

Working his way through the overgrown landscape he found himself to spiritually be in, he searched for any sign of 'life'. Nothing. He called out to Alice. "Alice, I need to meet with you, and talk with you.   Are you there?"   Still nothing.   He repeated himself, and silently also asked his guides to bring her forth if they could.   At first the vines seemed heavier than before, but finally they gave way to swampland that had large trees growing on grassy mounds, but he had to be very careful where he stepped to avoid the watery channels everywhere.   He stepped onto a higher than usual knoll and stopped to look around him. He could see in all directions; there were more gnarled trees, swampland and on the horizon, heavy grey and red streaked skies. It was impossible to tell if it was day or night – the air was heavy with damp and he thought it smelled of dead carcasses.

"Alice, I am here to *talk* with you, that is all.   Please join me for a conversation. I need to help you understand what is happening to you and your body, and what will happen when your body dies. Alice, I'm not here to hurt you or any part of you."

He waited again, and still no reply.   Finally, he thought he detected movement out of the corner of his eye.   He waited as quietly as a hunter not wanting to startle a deer. As she moved into view he remained very still, wanting her to feel that she was in charge of their meeting. He looked at her eventually as she stood before him and was a little surprised. The Alice she allowed him to see was very beautiful at first glance. Full bodied, long hair, and a proud stance. This was not a weak, dying woman who had let herself become aged and frail. Here was a warrior, ready to battle to the death. He was a little afraid it might come to that as he looked at her, carefully deciding what to say.

"You look well."

"Why do you care?"

"Your physical self is dying. It's very close to the end."

"I know that old man. I'm not afraid of it. In fact, I welcome it. Then I can become this." She waved her hands beautifully along the length of her body then put them on her hips, undulating slightly. Oh yes, she knew her power. He knew it was not real.

"When you die, you will not be able to sustain 'this'." He indicated her statuesque appearance with the flick of one hand. His cavalier attitude served to inflame her, he could see that, but her sudden concern over his words calmed her too.

"When Alice dies, I can go anywhere, be anyone. I am Hashihime, and I am all powerful. Don't you know me old man?"

"Of course I do. We've travelled together for several years now, and you know I'm not afraid of you. I am afraid *for* you though. Your sense of power is not real and you will not last long with Alice as your vehicle."

Alice's eyes grew dark and she raised herself up to her full height. "What would you know old man? Nothing!"

Yuki casually shrugged his shoulders. "I know I can help you if you'll let me. But first, what is it about Petra that has you so passionate and focused. She must mean nothing to you surely? Alice, might have reason to despise her maybe, but you, powerful Hashihime have no lasting need to focus your energy on any one person."

"Petra is like all women who think they can take who is not theirs for the taking, she must be destroyed so others may know of my power. It's been far too quiet lately. Besides, it's fun!"

"You have overestimated yourself this time. Let me help you?" Yuki was determined to undermine her confidence in the plan she had created for herself. But she seemed resolute. It was time to drive home his advantage.

"Hashihime, you have not yet tried this before, I have seen how this will work. You will end up stuck between two worlds if Alice's body dies before you have completed your transformation." He hoped he was right – but had no way of knowing for sure.

He sensed her hesitation, but before he could go any further she tossed her hair and stormed away. There was nothing further he could do for now and allowed himself to return to the hospital room and Alice's bedside where James was watching him intently.

CHAPTER 30

James and Yuki sat quietly and waited for the girl to appear with their tea. The hospital garden café was quiet, and the fading afternoon sun left a lingering warmth in the courtyard. Once their tea was poured, Yuki finally began to speak.

"I've met with the demon who is taking over your wife's mind and body. Her name is indeed Hashihime, and she is the demon goddess of jilted lovers. You are already aware of the story of how she came to be. But what you may not be aware of is her power to take over a well person and effectively suck the life out of them."

"I believe that Alice may have decided to study the Hashihime during the time she was first diagnosed as unwell and perhaps her mental agility was also affected by then, or maybe the Hashihime was the cause of her mental decline. Either way, the Hashihime has 'stolen' her way into your wife's body, and mind, and is growing more powerful as both your wife and your... Petra... is she your lover? I hate to ask, but I feel it's important to know under the circumstances."

"Petra and I love each other deeply and yes we are lovers. But only for about three months," confessed James.

"Ok, well that makes little difference really. But it's good to know. The Hashihime plays on the jealousy your wife has experienced during your marriage – perhaps there was another? James shook his head and sipped his tea, hoping the old man believed him.

Yuki continued, "The biggest challenge is that we need to stop the Hashihime from going any further at all in her quest to become powerful before Alice dies. Once that happens, her ability to transfer her power fully into Petra, or any other living woman is a very real possibility. She has already managed to get into Petra's head so to speak, I believe the next phase of this transformation is to jump from where she resides currently in Alice's fragile form, then jump across to Petra in order to continue her ability to 'live' in the real world."

"How can we do that?" asked James, his voice trembling at the thought of what that might mean.

"Petra needs to push back. I'm hoping she's strong enough and we'll have to guide her through it, but I have some experience with this type of thing. So long as she fully understands the risk, we can do it I think."

"Wait a minute, what risk? And what do you mean 'you think'?" James replaced his cup in the saucer and both men noticed the rattle as he shook.

Yuki's heart went out to the man in front of him as he contemplated the acute levels of stress he must be experiencing. Leaning over he took his hand and held it for the briefest of moments before replying. "There is a risk that we might fail. We also might lose Petra?"

"What do you mean 'lose her'?"

Yuki smiled sadly and said simply, "She might die too."

"Oh my God." James sat with that thought for a long minute. Tears welled up in his eyes and he squeezed them shut, hoping to prevent them spilling out. He failed, and Yuki again felt the strongest compassion for him.

"But we might succeed too. We have to think about that, and we have to work quickly. I can see that Alice might have no more than twenty-four hours to live at best. I would like to propose a bedtime vigil through the night with all of us. The hospital staff will most likely allow it, as it is the final hours of her life and you are her husband. We can easily explain Petra as being her sister or other close relative, and then there's me, and I've already been in. The person this is going to affect the most is Petra. I'd like us to go and talk with her so I can explain what needs to be done."

James sat in stupefied silence for a very long minute, trying to take in all that had just been said. Finally, he concluded he had nothing to lose and everything to gain by trusting the old man, but fear gripped his insides like a bear trap.

A short while later they were sitting with Mynda and Petra. Yuki explained the situation as clearly as he could, aware of the matter of time ticking.

"So what exactly are we going to do?" Petra felt very excited about the potential for ending this nightmare, so much so that she barely heard the warning about what they were about to do. James hadn't seen such enthusiasm for anything from her for such a long time he'd almost forgotten how beautiful she was when her eyes sparkled.

"We're going to sit with her, and we'll all hold hands to ensure strength for you most of all. I'll take you through a guided meditation to the place we'll meet the 'new' Alice, who is now unrecognisable as Alice I have to say. She looks more like an Amazonian Warrior from centuries ago. As the Hashihime, she's very dangerous, but we have to remember – all of us – that she is a demon. She's energy, and a powerful energy too, but as with all energy, it can be manipulated. James, you must not let go of Petra's hand and you'll need to mentally send her every bit of love imaginable. Just keep pouring that into her at all costs. At the same time, I want you to project as much love as possible onto Alice."

"Ok. I'm up for that. Is it ok if it's not real? I mean I don't really feel a lot of love for her anymore – haven't for years."

"James, make sure you feel it and project it as much as you possibly can. The life of both Alice and Petra depends upon it. I can't stress how important it is that we exorcise the Hashihime before Alice physically dies."

Petra and James both nodded and he squeezed her hand in reassurance. "It's going to be ok my darling I promise you." Petra looked at him and smiled.

"Petra, when we meet with the Hashihime she will be mean, nasty, vile, and incredibly manipulative. She hates you, but wants to take over your body when Alice dies, so it's important for her to be reminded first that you need your strength, not to be weakened. I will also be talking to her while you are there, and you must not think about anything else but this." Yuki pushed his chair back from the table a little further and leaned both hands on the edge of it. "Just as I am pushing this table away from my body, I want you to imagine doing the same with your hands – but doing it in your mind. And I want you to think about pushing with a solid wall of love giving you strength to push as hard as possible. You'll be pushing against the Hashihime. Do you understand?"

"I think so" replied Petra.

Our only way to combat this is to push against her by giving her love. Demons and negative spirits can't handle love. It doesn't feed them – hatred and anger gives them a lot of power however. She will say things to make you waiver, and try to get you to hate her so she can feed off your own negative emotions." Petra nodded her understanding.

"Can Mynda come too?" Petra asked.

"Well I think that would be ideal, the more support and love we can bring into that room the better, but James, would the hospital staff think it strange that so many strangers are attending an all-night vigil for Alice?"

James thought about it for barely a moment before replying. "I think it will be fine.   Besides. What can they do – say no?"

CHAPTER 31

Alice's eyelids fluttered for a moment – her shallow breathing rattled a little - a sign of the end drawing near. She was no longer aware of the state of her physical being, but in her other world, she could feel her strength slowly starting to drain away. It had been a hard few days, and the unexpected visit from the Japanese man was unwelcome. In reality, Alice was no longer Alice, but a strange blend of demon spirit and resilient young Alice. Neither was aware of the potential outcome but both knew this state of suspension could not last.

As she pondered this, she felt her name being called. She drifted out to the swamplands where as Hashihime she liked to meet and play with Petra, her latest victim. There she found Petra standing quietly beside Yuki. Inwardly she cringed, outwardly she boldly moved towards them gathering as much of her strength as possible – knowing they were there to do their best to eliminate her.

"What do you want old man?" She moved as close as she could and raised herself up to a full height to look down at him. Petra stood beside him, holding firmly to his hand. Odd that she had come to visit rather than being dragged here by Alice. She put that thought to one side and focused on Yuki – she'd get to Petra soon enough.

Yuki stood calmly beside Petra, and squeezed her hand gently in reassurance. He refused to answer Alice, wanting to inspire her anger – angry, she would be weaker. That was his best strategy, and he hoped it would work. What he had not told James and Petra was that he'd only tried to do this one other time, and that he'd lost his own love in the process. He was confident of having learnt from that expensive lesson, but a measure of fear slipped down his spine.

Alice walked around them both, then sneered at him, before turning to Petra. "And you, you think you can escape me and yet here you are. Sleepy are you? Tired? Having bad dreams today? Let's see what we can do about that shall we?"

Petra had always shrunk in fear at her taunts up until now, but this time to Alice's utter amazement she looked straight at her and almost imperceptibly moved forward, eyes open, and calm as she met the Hashihime' s gaze. For the first time, Petra completely believed that this was not Alice anymore, but some other person who was totally focused on being destructive towards her. This gave her confidence to stand her ground and continue looking into Alice's eye – carefully not breaking the gaze. Petra remembered what Yuki had said and focused on feeling loving and sincere towards the other woman, and held fast to his hand.

She was also vaguely aware of James holding her hand physically as they sat around Alice's bed, and drew on that feeling of love he was doing his best to pour into her too. She knew he loved her, as she loved him. They had a chance for happiness, and Alice was dying. There was nothing anyone could do about that now, and her strange behaviour of the past few years was not of Petra's making. She finally knew with absolute certainty that she had nothing at all to feel guilty about. His marriage had been over for years… he was a good man staying to nurse his wife to the end, but that did not mean that she, Petra was stealing him away from Alice. He had emotionally exited the relationship long before they found each other again.

As she stood before the woman that Alice was becoming, or had become, she knew that she was in grave danger. There was a real chance that Alice might die at any time and if that happened before they finished this mission, then the Hashihime might take over Petra's mind and body just as she had found a gateway into Alice's physical and mental self some time ago. But Petra also trusted James and Yuki, and as she focused on pouring feelings of love into the version of Alice standing before them both, she felt herself growing a little stronger.

Yuki broke the silence at last. "You didn't think I'd just go away did you Alice?"

Alice finally broke eye contact with Petra and looked at him instead. Turning her head to one side like a marionette, she scoffed at him. "You! You think you can 'fix' me do you old man?" I can smell the fear in you... you are out of your depth here. I know I can take her – you can't stop me. Watch this!"

Suddenly she was above them both, starring down and screaming at them. Petra closed her eyes but only for a moment, then continued her task of thinking only loving thoughts and harmony, doing her very best to direct these feelings towards the demented woman screaming down at her.

Alice circled about them rising and stirring up the smells and sounds of the swamp. She circled, then danced about in a frenzy of motion, all the while screaming at them both. Yuki started chanting, a strange series of sounds that were unfamiliar to either of the women, but as he did so, he seemed to grow a little taller, and strength poured from him to match the love being projected by Petra. Together their energy started to affect the momentum of the Hashihime. Her screaming became softer, as she started to fade.

Was it Petra's imagination or was Alice slowing down and becoming a less vibrant being? She kept tight hold of Yuki and continued to pour forth love and light. For the first time, she felt immune to the rants and raves of Alice, and as she did so, her love for herself grew. She could feel the power inside of herself starting to glow like a soft flame. She could do this – beat the eccentricities of this demonising bitch!

Then Petra smiled at Alice. A full, glowing, beautiful smile. And everything changed.

As Alice felt that love from her arch rival, she felt her own strength diminish further. She could no longer levitate and dance above her opponents, and sank back to ground level. The stench of the swamp receded, and the light began to prickle the back of her eyes. "You can't have him. I'll stop you. I'll always be there to stop you. He's mine – not yours, and he needs to be with me. He was never yours, always mine. Always mine. You can't have him…"

Her voice grew weaker and her colours continued to fade. Petra was no longer sure if she was looking at the Hashihime or at Alice, but she could easily sense the difference taking place. Alice was starting to look more and more like the woman lying on the hospital bed in the room they were in. The magnificent creature they'd encountered on arrival was departing. Yuki knew it was all about energy and he continued to chant and direct positive energy towards Alice. Soon, he knew it was nearly over. He could feel the change, but he wanted to be sure. There was no room for error this time.

Finally, Alice – the real Alice – stood before them both. Tears welled up in her eyes, as she kept saying quietly, "he's mine… he's mine… he's mine."

"Alice, is that you?" Yuki stopped chanting and gently asked the question. She stopped her own chanting and looked at him for a long moment before answering.

"Yes." Her voice was now barely a whisper. And she resembled a frail child, scared and alone in the marshes of a barren land.

"Alice, we don't want to hurt you. We are here to help you. Do you know that you are dying?"

Alice nodded slowly. A tear silently slipped down her cheek.

"It will be ok. You can rest knowing that your wishes will be followed, your daughter and granddaughter will be safe and loved by James, and James will always honour the love you shared for many years. You have lived a good life, and the future is brighter than you can even imagine. You can rest now. Ok?" Yuki spoke to her as he would have a frightened child and she seemed to respond well. "Alice, is the Hashihime gone?"

"I don't know."

"Let me tell you about her before we see shall we?" She nodded again. "The Hashihime was seeking a way to stay here, through you, and after you would die, she would find another victim, this time it would be Petra. Alice, do you understand that we, you, me, Petra, and everyone around you, needs to have her gone from your life, before you die."

Alice looked confused, so Yuki asked again. "Do you understand Alice? If she stays here with you, you can't have peace and a beautiful future when you leave this life. She will stay with you, and Petra, and then another victim. Alice, it's time for the Hashihime to leave and be allowed to find peace herself. Ok Alice?"

Alice nodded, and looked back at Petra. "I'm sorry," was all she whispered, and then she was gone.

Yuki looked at Petra and guided her gently but quickly out of their deep meditation and back to the hospital room. Petra opened her eyes slowly and squeezed James' hand. She smiled at him and nodded. Mynda felt the change in the room and opened her eyes too, looking around at the others, then at Alice. "Oh!" she said quietly.

The woman lying on the bed was not the same woman they'd seen earlier. This Alice was quite simply, beautiful as she lay there.

Her skin no longer waxen, and her breathing was still shallow but the rattle had subsided. She almost glowed with good health. James looked at Petra and then at Yuki, with eyebrows raised, wondering what on earth this meant, before he pressed the buzzer for the nurse.

Nurse Addison and Doctor Yates entered moments later. Checking Alice's vital signs and chart, they looked at each other in evident surprise before Dr Yates spoke to the group. "Well what ever prayer's you've been saying over our patient this last hour, something's working. Alice's vital signs are a little improved and she's resting comfortably again. I'm not sure exactly what this means, but it's a good thing. I am confident she'll have a peaceful night ahead, so you can all either keep doing what you're doing, or go and rest yourselves till morning."

With that he left the room, leaving a nurse behind to continue to monitor Alice throughout the night.

James indicated they should all leave and he bent over his resting wife and kissed her on the forehead and squeezed her hand before he followed them. They all waited until they were back at the hotel before talking about what had happened. James and Mynda said they had felt something odd in the air while Yuki and Petra were 'away' but couldn't really describe it. Yuki and Petra did their best to explain what they had experienced to the others.

"The question remains, was it successful?" Yuki tapped his long fingers on the table, quietly contemplating the last few hours, hoping that this had worked out well, but still a little nervous about the potential for the Hashihime to have stayed on. She most likely had left Alice, but that was not definite yet. And he didn't think she had taken over Petra just yet – she seemed much stronger and calmer too. "Only time will tell."

He suddenly yawned, and embarrassed, put his hand over his face. "Please tell me where I can sleep. I'm sorry but it's been a very long and intense day. And my internal time clock suggests it's nearly time to get up."

"Of course, I'll take you to your room – we've got you a suite upstairs," said James. He kissed Petra gripped Petra's hand, promising to return in a few minutes, and said goodnight to Mynda. Mynda left too, and Petra found herself alone with her thoughts.

She felt calm for the first time in weeks. The tension in the back of her neck seemed to have left her, and her head felt too heavy for her body. Exhaustion was taking over her body much the same way as Yuki seemed to have physically crashed into that state a few moments earlier. She moved across the room and sat on the edge of the bed, thinking back briefly over what Alice had said to her."

When James arrived back in the room fifteen minutes later, he found her stretched across the bed, snoring softly, deeply asleep. He lay down beside her and put his arm around her, smiled, then dropped off too.

EPILOGUE

10 days later, Petra met James at the door, unsure whether it was appropriate to look happy or not – should she conceal the delight inside her at the thought Alice was no longer a part of their lives? Alice had still held on for three days after Yuki's visit, but had finally died peacefully with James, Brett, and Deanna in the room. Maddie had declared she was too upset to actually watch her grandmother die.

"How was it?"

"Well, there were a few people there… mostly it was just a cold, miserable way to spend an afternoon. Don and Mary were there, Brett said some nice things, and Deanna and Maddie were suitably upset. We'll be able to pick up the ashes in about a week."

"Do you think it's over now?"

"What do you mean?" James kissed the top of her forehead and dropped his keys on the table, before reaching into the fridge for a cold bottle of water.

"Well, how will we know if she's going to somehow continue to bother us from 'the other side'? Yuki Masimoto seemed to be a little uncertain about the end results really. Well I thought so anyway."

Petra pulled out a barstool from the breakfast area and perched half sitting on it, like a bird ready to take flight at a moment's notice. She was trying hard to be calm, but there remained a feeling of terror deep inside that the nightmare might only be temporarily over. The thought of enduring more of Alice/Hashihime' s threatening antics was almost more than she could bear, and had made her consider carefully, how she felt about James and whether she might love him enough to live with any further issues from Alice, even after her death.

James put his water bottle down, and came over to her, pulling her to a standing position and hugged her deeply, warmly, and then kissed her slowly, gently with increasing passion. "I love you Petra Walsh. I love you more than you could even begin to imagine. If there is ever, anything at all that even slightly looks like a return of my wife or her bloody demons I'll personally learn everything I can about waging all-out war on them all so that you, my dearest wonderful Petra are safe. Is that what you need to know?" He nuzzled her neck, loving the feel of her light weight in his arms.

"That is exactly all I need to know... and I love you too. Very much. I'm sure we'll be able to handle anything at all that ever comes up for us in the future, won't we." She hesitated for a moment and then said the one thing that made the hairs on the back of his neck stand up – just a little. "Anything but infidelity aye!" Her eyes met his and she smiled, before turning away.

James looked at the back of her head, then reached for his water bottle. 'Wow', he thought silently. I need to watch that I don't read too much into things maybe. He shook his head and sighed.

ACKNOWLEDGEMENTS

Thanks first to the lovely Karen, Lynnette, and Debby who read through the early drafts of this story and whose enthusiasm and encouragement helped me to focus on finishing this novel.

To Richard who happily tolerated my endless desire to write, even while we were on holiday, as the story unfolding became an obsession.

Thanks to Bronwyn for her excellent editing and review.

Finally – thanks to a particularly complex lady for all the inspiration to start this story. I wish her nothing but peace and love in the next round.

OTHER WORKS OF FICTION BY DIXIE CARLTON

A Song Out of Time – the Margaret McKenzie Story

Beyond the Shadows

OTHER WORKS OF NON-FICTION BY (DIXIE) MARIA CARLTON

The Taboo Conversations/That Sex Book

Golden Nuggets

Advertising, Branding, Marketing 101

From Idea to Authority

The Power of Promotional Products (with David Blaise)

It's Not All Just Junk (with Richard Macdonald)

20/20 – A Fresh Look at... - Series (with Terry Hawkins, Keith Abraham, Ann Andrews Et Al)

The Power of More Than One - Series (Collaborative) with Pat Mesiti, Paul Tonich, Terry Hawkins Et Al)

ABOUT DIXIE CARLTON

Dixie is a full-time writer and coach currently living in Brisbane, but was born, raised, and lived most of her life in New Zealand. An insatiable curiosity about 'just about everything', she often turns her experiences, conversations and interesting people into stories or characters.

When she's not traveling, writing, or taking photos, she's usually found taking a break at the movies, reading, kayaking, or hanging out with a handful of her favorite people.

www.dixiecarlton.com

www.facebook.com/dixiecarltonauthor

www.twitter.com/dixiecarlton

www.instagram.com/curatingconversations

Please follow Dixie's author page for updates on new titles coming.

www.amazon.com/author/dixiecarlton

EXCERPT FROM

BEYOND THE SHADOWS

The fog was so thick, she could barely breathe and wondered if maybe she was having an asthma attack – not that she'd ever had one before. Trying to draw breathe at all felt like she was sucking it through a thick blanket. As she moved, she was slowed down by the inability to fill her lungs sufficiently, and then noticed that she couldn't see more than a few feet in front of her anyway. Running would be useless she realised, and then stopped suddenly. "But where am I anyway? This is the weirdest dream I've ever had." She was not entirely sure if she was dreaming, or awake, thinking out loud or actually speaking. This was like the dreams she could remember having as a small child when she was never sure if they were real – but it was like dreaming you are having a dream. The blurred lines of reality were like train tracks, lying side by side, separate but still maintained together in the one track.

A ticking clock grew louder as the darkness increased. Turning around, she thought she could reach out and touch it, but then when she tried to do so, the clock turned into a bird, squawking a warning as it swooped over her head. She felt it, but could see nothing. "There you go, Penny, you are just dreaming about the Ravens from the Tower tour today." The conscious part of her mind that seemed to know she was actually caught in a dream hissed at her sarcastically. The bird flew back across her head – lifting her hair this time it was so close. She put her hand up to her head to smooth her hair and felt the warm and sticky liquid, oozing through her fingers. She tried to hold her fingers in front of her face to see what the sticky substance was, but everything was completely black by now. Feeling once again to the top of her head, the liquid was increasing – it was starting to run down onto her face, and she could no longer feel her hair on the top of her head, only a warm mushy squishiness. In an instant she knew it was her brain she was feeling. "NO, wake up now, Penny you have to wake up - this is a dream and you have to wake up."

She tried to wake herself up but the deeper the darkness became the more it felt like she was being smothered by it. "Penny, you have to scream now – otherwise you'll never wake up again. *Scream, Penny!*" She was screaming the words to herself as her head continued to open up and cascading brains poured out and over her shoulders. "Scream yourself awake NOW Penny, NOW before it's too late." She could hear herself getting louder and louder, as the darkness obscured everything but the vision of her head peeling back and erupting like a volcano.

This book and others are available on Amazon and other leading online book stores – as print and ebook options. You can find out more at:

www.amazon.com/author/dixiecarlton